THE BIG KILL

book nine of the matchmaker mysteries series

elise sax

The Big Kill (Matchmaker Mysteries – Book 9) is a work of fiction. Names, characters, places, and incidents are the products of the author's imagination or are used fictitiously. Any resemblance to actual events, locales, or persons, living or dead, is entirely coincidental.

ISBN: 978-1985705739
Published in the United States by 13 Lakes Publishing

Cover design: Elizabeth Mackey
Edited by: Novel Needs
Formatted by: Jesse Kimmel-Freeman

Printed in the United States of America

elisesax.com
elisesax@gmail.com
Newsletter: https://bit.ly/2PzAhRx
https://www.facebook.com/ei.sax.9

For Meital

ALSO BY ELISE SAX

Matchmaker Mysteries Series

Matchmaking Advice from Your Grandma Zelda

Road to Matchmaker

An Affair to Dismember

Citizen Pain

The Wizards of Saws

Field of Screams

From Fear to Eternity

West Side Gory

Scareplane

It Happened One Fright

The Big Kill

It's a Wonderful Knife

Ship of Ghouls

Matchmaker Marriage Mysteries

Gored of the Rings

Slay Misty for Me

Scar Wars

Goodnight Mysteries Series

Die Noon

A Doom with a View

Jurassic Dark

Coal Miner's Slaughter

Wuthering Frights

Agatha Bright Mysteries Series

The Fear Hunter

Some Like It Shot

Fright Club

Beast of Eden

Creepy Hollow

Partners in Crime Series

Partners in Crime

Conspiracy in Crime

Divided in Crime

Surrender in Crime

Operation Billionaire Trilogy

How to Marry a Billionaire

How to Marry Another Billionaire

How to Marry the Last Billionaire on Earth

Five Wishes Series

Five Wishes Series

Going Down

Man Candy

Hot Wired

Just Sacked

Wicked Ride

Three More Wishes Series

Blown Away

Inn & Out

Quick Bang

Three More Wishes Series

Standalone Books

Forever Now

Bounty

Switched

CHAPTER 1

Remember that a match is the sum of his parts, bubbeleh. I'm talking about his past. Just because you don't see it, doesn't mean it's not eating at him like Marty Goldblatt working through a brisket sandwich. Forget it, let go, leave it behind...this is the advice we're all given. It's good advice, but impossible to do. Kind of like losing weight and getting more sleep. Impossible. Without a doubt, your match is going to have something in his past that's affecting his chances for love. Bad father, bully in second grade, the list goes on. So, be patient with your matches, dolly. Dig a little and try to find the truth. For sure, you'll find a shocking something in their past. You can't fix it, you can't change what's already happened, but you can understand, and understanding is the key to love.

Lesson 77, Matchmaking advice from your Grandma Zelda

Everything I thought I knew about my life changed during one day in June, and it all started because I was determined to finally organize my Grandma Zelda's matchmaking business.

That's why I was sitting in her attic, sneezing.

"I'm not allergic to dust," I told myself and sneezed, loudly again, sending a small pile of scrap paper flying off a folding table to the floor. So much for the power of positive thinking.

I had started organizing her "files" almost a year before, but I had given up in the face of the impossible. Now I was at it again, and this time I was determined, like a guy climbing Mt. Everest, even though his nose might freeze and fall off. My grandmother must have sensed my determination because she had given me a new laptop for the project. The computer was sitting on the table, along with stacks of old papers and notecards, after I had tried for hours to figure out how to create an Excel spreadsheet.

I never figured it out.

I had recently begun to have some success as a matchmaker, and I guessed organizing the business was part of me finally staking ownership as my grandmother's partner. Either that, or I was hiding in the attic from my fiancé.

Spencer Bolton was the love of my life. And he was hot. And he believed that I should have an orgasm before he had an orgasm. So, in other words, he was perfect. Not to mention that he had bought me a house across the street, and he wanted to marry me in one month.

One month.

In one month, I would be living in a big house with a pool—that I *owned*--and a husband for as long as we both shall live.

My heart beat loudly in my chest, and I took my pulse to make sure I wasn't dying. My pulse was fast, but I had lost track counting the beats, so I took a swig from my beer bottle. I wasn't normally a drinker, but thinking about a house and a husband had driven me to consuming domestic beer on the sly in the attic while I was hiding. I mean, organizing.

Dropping to the floor, I crawled to the little window and snuck a peek outside. Across the street, Spencer was standing on the sidewalk with the contractor, and he was waving his arms around. The contractor was nodding his head back at him. There was an army of construction workers going in and out of the house like ants. Spencer had insisted on a double team of workers, striving toward a strict deadline, two days before our wedding.

I had never seen Spencer more excited about anything than he was about building a custom-made house. Ordering the plate warmer for the kitchen had sent him over the moon. I had made the mistake of telling him I didn't care about paint colors or bamboo flooring when the renovations started, and Spencer took it as a statement on my love and devotion to him. In other words, he moped. So, since then I pretended to be thrilled about mini-blinds and garage doors. But the truth was that blueprints and decorating just made me want to drink cheap beer and hide.

I watched through the window as Spencer scratched the back of his neck and then turned around, looking up. I dropped down to the floor, hoping he hadn't caught me spying on him. On my tombstone, it was going to read: *Here lies Gladie Burger, coward.* Or would it say, *Here lies Gladie Bolton*? I hadn't thought about changing my name. Was that expected?

I crawled back to the table, grabbed the bottle of beer, and drank the rest. It didn't help. I was still engaged.

Pushing a pile of papers aside, I lifted a box onto the table and sneezed. Just like the other boxes, it was old and crammed with papers and notebooks. But the handwriting was not my grandmother's. I recognized my mother's handwriting, and she had written my father's name on the side of it.

I sucked in air and stopped breathing. Everything I had found in the attic up until that moment had to do with matchmaking. From reading my grandmother's chicken scratch notes on yellowed notecards and scraps of paper, I had learned more about every resident of our small town of Cannes, California than their therapists and mothers.

And there were notes and notebooks in the attic that went further back than my grandmother. They went all the way back to the first woman in our family to be a matchmaker in town, who built her dream house—the house I was living in-- during the founding of Cannes in the late 19th century, much like Spencer was building our dream house today.

"John West wants a woman with blond hair, but he'll take any woman who still has her front teeth," the first matchmaker had written in one notebook entry. The beautiful handwriting was barely legible because the pencil marks had become faded and smudged in the more than one hundred years since it had been written. I had put all of these kinds of notebooks in a plastic bin, but I had decided to throw out the scraps of paper. More recent business I put aside to organize later.

But this was the first time I had seen anything with my father's name on it and the first time I had seen my mother's handwriting on anything in the attic. My father had died when I was a little girl in a motorcycle accident, and his death destroyed my family. My grandmother became a shut in, and my mother became a drunk and threw away her responsibilities as a mother. If I had been a little more introspective, I would have drawn a line from my father's death to my commitment issues, but beer was better than introspection.

I picked up the beer bottle but then remembered that it was empty. Taking a deep breath, I began to open the box with my father's name on it, but my phone rang, and I answered. It was Bridget.

"It's time!" she shouted into the phone, hyperventilating. "It's...it's...it's...time! Did you hear me? Are you there? Gladie! Gladie! It's time! Run through the stop signs! Take Spencer's police car and turn on the siren! It's time!"

"Are you sure?" I asked, softly.

"Don't you think I know when it's time? It's time! Get your butt over here before…oh ooh waw!"

I broke out into a sweat, and my heart raced. "I'm coming!" I shouted into the phone. "Don't do anything until I get you to a hospital!"

"Ooooohhhh! It's happening!"

I high-tailed it out of the attic, tripping over boxes. "It's happening!" I yelled, as I made it down the stairs and ran to my bedroom, where I got my purse and then ran down the stairs again to the bottom floor. My grandmother was in the parlor with her friend, Meryl, the blue-haired librarian. The house had been relatively quiet since the Easter egg hunt debacle two months before in April. Since then, volunteerism had taken a nosedive, probably because volunteers had a good dose of post-Easter PTSD. "It's happening!" I shouted. "Bridget's in labor!"

"Again?" Meryl asked.

"She says it's real now," I said.

"That's what she said yesterday," Meryl pointed out.

"And the day before yesterday," Grandma said.

"And the day before that," Meryl added. "Guess what. Zelda found a great caterer for your wedding party. He makes pizza with caviar. Doesn't that sound good?"

It sounded delicious except for the caviar part. My grandmother had been handling the wedding, while I was hiding.

"You and Spencer are such a romantic couple," Meryl continued. "You're just like Prince Charles and Lady Di."

"Meryl, it didn't turn out well for Charles and Diana, you know," I said.

"What're you talking about? They had a beautiful wedding. I have a commemorative plate."

My phone rang, again. It was Bridget. "I'm coming!" I yelled into the phone. "Gotta go," I told my grandmother and Meryl as I ran outside.

"Pinky, you want to put your two cents in about wainscoting?" Spencer called from across the street, as I fumbled with my car keys.

"Wainscoting? I thought he was great in the last Star Trek movie," I called back. "Bridget's in labor. Gotta go!"

"Again?"

I sped out of the driveway and through the Historic District to Bridget's townhouse. Luckily, I had only drunk one beer over three hours, and I was still sober. That didn't stop me from running over a couple of curbs on my way to her home. When I got there, she was waiting for me on the sidewalk. She was wearing a blue pregnancy muumuu with her hand between her legs, as if she was planning on catching the baby before it hit the ground.

"It's happening!" she shouted, and I screeched to a stop in front of her. I jumped out of the car and helped her into the car. "Step on it! It's happening!"

I hopped back in the car and stepped on it, and we got to the hospital in less than three minutes. Bridget kept her hand between her legs as we walked through the parking lot and didn't move it when we entered the maternity ward. "It's happening!" she shouted.

"Again?" the nurse at the front desk asked.

Bridget slapped her free hand on the desk. "Get me a wheelchair and wheel me into exam room number one. Dr. Sara is on her way." Her voice sounded like she was starring in *The Exorcist.* She was terrifying. I was expecting green vomit to spew from her mouth and her head to spin around at any moment. The nurses were scared, too, and they jumped into action.

By the time that Bridget was settled in the exam room, dressed in a hospital gown that tied in the back, Dr. Sara arrived. Dr. Sara wasn't actually a doctor. She was a woo-woo, la-la person who delivered babies, unless there was trouble and then she called for a real doctor. I was very suspicious of Dr. Sara. Maybe it was because of her heavy reliance on Reiki for pain or maybe it was the music she brought with her on her Alexa machine every time that Bridget thought she was in labor.

"Alexa, tambourines," she commanded sweetly, putting the Alexa speaker down next to Bridget's bed. Tambourine noises started, and Dr. Sara touched Bridget's shoulder and smiled serenely. "How is the daughter of the Earth Mother doing?"

"A baby is going to squeeze out of my vagina. How do you think I'm doing?" Bridget screeched and did her Lamaze panting-breathing. I wished I had brought beer with me. I wished Bridget hadn't picked me as her labor coach. I was supposed to be coaching, but instead, I was gnawing at a cuticle and sweating through my shirt.

"You want ice chips?" I asked her, finally remembering the classes I went to with Bridget. "You want me to massage your lower back? Maybe you should get an epidural. Epidurals are good, Bridget."

She shook her head. "Epidurals aren't natural, Gladie. My baby's going to be natural. You don't want my baby to be unnatural, do you? Besides, look how wonderfully I'm handling the pain. I'm like a Zen master with the pain. I've practiced for this, and I'm one with the pain. One with the—Oooh! Sonofabitch! Yowza! Ow! Motherfucker!" she shouted, hitting the bed with her fists. She took a deep breath and turned back toward me. "So, I'm totally fine. No pain medication for me. I am--Ooooh! Here it comes, again! Holy hell! The pain! The pain!" Bridget shouted.

The tambourine music kept playing, and Dr. Sara kept smiling. She wasn't panicking at all. Meanwhile, I was biting down on my hand. In that instant, it dawned on me that Bridget was going to have an actual baby. A human being was going to come into this world because Bridget pushed it out. And I was the coach!

"Here it comes!" I shouted, panic mixing with excitement in me.

"Let's take a little peek at our wondrous addition to the universe," Dr. Sara sang, raising Bridget's knees. I turned around to give Bridget her privacy. "I see. I see. Uh huh.

Okay. You can put your legs down, now, Bridget."

I took that as my cue to turn back around.

"Alexa, flutes," Dr. Sara instructed and smiled at Bridget. "Another little false alarm. These things happen," she said, but I noticed she was struggling to keep her patience. This trip to the hospital made seven false alarms in five days. I didn't know much about pregnancy, but I was getting the impression that seven false alarms wasn't normal.

"Look, again, Dr. Sara. I can feel the contraction," Bridget urged, turning her pelvis so that Dr. Sara could get an eye-full. "It's happening right now, and if I push…" Bridget gave a little grunt, and instead of a baby shooting out of her pelvis, she farted. "Oh, that feels better," she said and farted again. Her face changed from pain to relief to realization to humiliation.

"Gas is a perfectly normal side effect of bearing life," Dr. Sara said, nonchalantly covering her nose. "Alexa, stop music."

We knew the drill from there. Dr. Sara left after bestowing a Sanskrit blessing on Bridget, and I helped my best friend get dressed. It was on the tip of my tongue to point out to her that if gas pains were going to drive her to screams, I didn't think she was going to make it through labor without an epidural. But somehow—maybe survival instinct--I kept my mouth shut. If it were me, and I was having a baby, I would get an epidural, a couple margaritas, and whatever drugs I could buy on the street corner.

At the thought of labor, my heart raced. If I wasn't

ready to talk about bamboo flooring, I sure wasn't ready to think about babies. Although a baby with Spencer would be so cute. Spencer would dress him in little baseball outfits and teach him to throw a ball, and I would…I would…what would I do?

"I want deep fried gummy worms," Bridget told me, standing face to face, her expression complete defeat.

"Deep fried gummy worms?"

"And I want them now. I need them, Gladie. I'm on my last nerve. They're sold at one place in town."

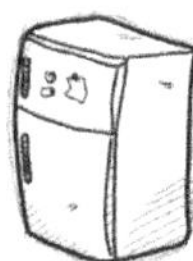

Deep fried gummy worms were sold at Mart-n-Save, the mini-mart near the park. Bridget hadn't said a word on the drive there. I assumed she was slightly embarrassed by and a lot fed up with her false alarms. "You can wait in the car, and I'll go in," I told her, turning off the motor.

"Get Tums, too," she said. "I'll just sit here and fart."

"Good idea," I said and opened her window.

Inside, the clerk was a twenty-something man with greasy hair and a pimply face, and he was surfing through a nudie magazine next to the vertical hot dog spinner. "Do you have deep-fried gummy worms?" I asked. Without looking up from his magazine, he pointed to a place behind me. I turned around and walked down the aisle.

I scanned the shelves of junk food, searching for

Bridget's treat, and bumped into a teenage boy, who was standing with two other boys around his age. All three were wearing matching T-shirts, which had DICK written on them, circled with a line struck through, like a No Smoking sign. The shirts looked they had been drawn with a Sharpie. No Dick? I figured it must have been a new hip hop band that I didn't know about because I hung around old people every day, when I wasn't hiding in an attic. I sighed and resolved to myself to stay young and current, somehow. At least, I decided, I would read Us Weekly and listen to hits radio from now on.

"Third shelf down," the boy told me. "Can you help us?"

"Are you in trouble?" I asked, looking around. It was just us and the cashier. The rest of the tiny store was empty, except for more than its share of dirt and grime and enough sugar to give all of Southern California diabetes.

"We're buying bubble gum," he told me with a smile and pointed to one of his friends, who was stuffing packets of bubble gum into his pockets. Stores no longer provided bags in California, and it was a problem.

"You're buying a lot of gum," I noted.

The boy shrugged. "Kids. What'cha gonna do?"

"We've got all of the gum down here, but there's a bunch in the back that we can't reach. Will you help?"

"But you're taller than I am," I said. They were taller. They were about sixteen years old and had reached or were near full-grown.

"You can climb on my shoulders," the first boy said.

"Don't they have a ladder?"

"They won't let us use it," he whispered to me.

"We really need the gum," the third boy explained. "SATs, you know."

I didn't know. I had never taken the SAT. I had never even finished high school. But maybe they needed to chew gum to study for or take the SAT. I didn't know, and I didn't want to ask because I was embarrassed that I didn't know. Besides, who was I to stand in the way of three young men and their education?

I followed them to the storage room, which was the size of a large shower. "See?" the first boy said, pointing to the highest shelf. Sure enough, there was a stack of three boxes of bubble gum.

"That shouldn't be too hard," I said, not sounding very convinced. "Are you sure you need all of that gum?"

"You can get on my shoulders, grab the gum, and you'll be down in two minutes, tops," the first boy said, and crouched down.

"That shouldn't be too hard," I repeated, still not sounding very convinced. I straddled the boy's shoulders, and he stood up, like I weighed nothing, which thrilled me and gave me new motivation to help them out. I stretched my arm and grabbed the top box.

"Throw it down," one of the boys urged. I tossed it to him and tossed the other boy the second box.

"What are you doing?" the cashier came into the

storage room and shouted, waving a gun at us. "Bubble gum bandits! Bubble gum bandits!"

"They're taking the SAT," I explained, staring down the barrel of his gun.

"They're the bubble gum bandits! I've already called the police. DICK! DICK! DICK!" the cashier shouted.

It had degenerated very fast.

"This can all be explained," I said, but he had stopped listening to me. Two of the boys ran like the wind out of the storage room while still holding the bubble gum that I had tossed to them. The cashier waved his gun at them, but thankfully, he didn't shoot. The boy underneath me shoved my legs off his shoulders and ran for it. I grabbed onto a shelf so I wouldn't fall.

A responsible shopkeeper will put safety first and bolt his shelves into the wall to avoid disastrous accidents. Especially in earthquake country, the shelves should be bolted in place. But the owner of Mart-n-Save didn't know about safety or didn't care because the shelves in the storage room weren't bolted into the wall.

So, when the boy underneath me shook me off and I grabbed on to the shelves for dear life, the shelves came down, like a domino filled with junk food. "Oh my God!" the cashier yelled, as boxes of Snickers and Pop-Tarts hit him in the face. He tried to shield his head with his gun, but it was of no use. The shelves toppled over and I swung my legs to try to catch my balance to save myself.

It was no use. The shelves, the junk food, and I came

tumbling down. The cashier must have had a strong jaw because it wasn't until I kicked him in the side of the head that he actually lost consciousness.

CHAPTER 2

There are a lot of rules about dating, and sooner or later, your matches will break all of them, bubbeleh. But if they remember to smile and give their date a compliment, it can't go all wrong. Practice a few compliments with them before they go out. For instance, maybe it's not so good to focus a compliment on their date's mole. "The mole on your nose isn't that bad," isn't the best compliment. Also, stay away from how fat or skinny they are or how straight their teeth are. Romantic compliments, those are not. Finding a good compliment isn't rocket science. Even if they're dating Quasimodo, they can find something about his sense of humor that's worth commenting on. You get what I'm saying, dolly? Find the positive in the match and make the experience positive.

Lesson 131, Matchmaking advice from your Grandma Zelda

"I'm in one piece," I said, amazed, touching myself. "Not a scratch on me."

The cashier didn't answer. He had broken my fall, and he was out cold. We were on the floor under a mountain of junk food and a lot of shelving. I heard police sirens coming closer. Two cop cars, and an ambulance was a few minutes behind them. I had become an expert at emergency vehicles.

"Hello, babe," I heard and craned my neck around to see Remington Cumberbatch, Spencer's detective, and my former casual sex partner. He was massive and sexy as hell, like The Rock but with more tattoos and an obsession for sci-fi movies. "Doing a little shopping?"

"They didn't bolt the shelves into the wall," I said.

Remington shook his head and tsked. "Don't they know we live in earthquake country?"

It was nice of him to focus on earthquakes, when Spencer would have wisecracked about me being the worst earthquake the town had ever experienced.

"Let me help you," Remington said.

"There's a man underneath me," I said.

Remington cracked a smile. "As I remember, that's your best position."

My face got hot and I probably turned a dark shade of purple, as my brain flashed through memories of Remington naked. He was a lot when he was naked. Like Naked Plus. Uber naked. Naked a la mode. Naked with a cherry on top. Naked, naked, naked.

I blinked out of my reverie, as Remington lifted the shelving off of me and leaned it against the wall, like it was nothing. He yanked me off of the cashier and put his hands on my shoulders, stabilizing me. He looked me in the eyes and smiled. He was very handsome.

And big.

"The boss is busy with wallpaper swatches, so Margie and I took the call," he told me, still holding on to me. His breath smelled of pizza, and my stomach growled. "And we're the bubble gum bandits' command force, so we had to come. Margie's upset that it cut into our lunch break."

The paramedics came in and examined the cashier, and Remington walked me back into the store with his arm draped over my shoulders.

"Margie's the new detective?" I asked.

Remington nodded. A woman in her fifties with a head of short, grey hair walked toward us. She was wearing a black pantsuit with more than her share of bulges and rolls, and I liked her immediately.

"Margie Lagler, detective," she said, introducing herself to me. "You were a witness to the bubble gum bandits?"

"When you say, bubble gum bandits..." I drifted off. I had to be careful. I didn't want to incriminate myself.

"Kids are running in gangs, stealing all of the bubble gum in town," Margie explained, shaking her head, as if the state of affairs in small town America made her sad.

"It's like a Scorsese movie," Remington commented and winked at me. I blushed, again, and felt guilty. Spencer wouldn't like me blushing at his detective and my former romp-in-the-hay-partner.

"That's terrible," I said, but my voice came out like Kermit the Frog, and I cleared it and looked away from Remington's twinkling eyes.

"Wha' happened?" the cashier groaned from inside the stock room.

"You got a bump on your head," one of the paramedics told him. "I don't think you have a concussion. You want me to take you to the hospital?"

"Is it free?" I heard the cashier ask. I already knew the answer to that.

Bridget waddled into the store. "What's going on? Gladie, didn't they have the gummy worms?"

"Oh, sorry. I got side-tracked." Because I was helping the bubble gum bandits rip off a convenience store. If it ever got back to Spencer, I would never hear the end of it. For some reason, he thought I was a troublemaker.

I showed Bridget where the deep-fried gummy worms were. She grabbed a package, ripped it open, and took a large bite. Her eyes closed in appreciation. "Being an earth goddess is a bitch," she moaned with her mouth full.

I didn't doubt it. I tried to avoid any earth goddess behavior whenever I could.

"I'm not giving you my name. You'll force me to pay you," the cashier yelled, marching out of the stockroom and side-stepping Remington and Margie. "You're paying for that, right?" he asked Bridget, who had started on her second package of worms.

"I'm a member of the ACLU," she told him, as if that explained things. "I'm going to need TUMS, too," Bridget whispered to me and belched. Her breath smelled like deep-fried gummy worms. I wanted to try one, but I didn't dare ask her to share. Pregnant women were scary about their cravings.

"I'll get you the TUMS and meet you at the front," I told her. I found them an aisle over and grabbed the biggest bottle.

Remington and Margie had followed the cashier, while the paramedics left the store. "We need a statement," Margie told him. "Can you describe the bubble gum bandits?"

"Three snot-nosed teenagers and her," he said, pointing at me. I crouched down behind the aisles.

It wasn't my proudest moment.

"Did you find more deep-fried gummy worms down there?" Bridget asked, looking down at me.

I swallowed and tried to gather my courage. Unfortunately, I didn't have a lot of courage to gather so after a few seconds of crouching, I stood up. Remington and Margie were staring at me, and the cashier was still pointing.

I put my hands on my hips. "Wha… huh… wha… muh… huh…?" I said, as if I was incredulous at the accusation that I was one of the bubble gum bandits.

"She kicked me in the head and fell on my face, too," the cashier continued. "Can you arrest her for that?"

Margie scratched her head. "Wait a minute. This is

the Gladie? The boss's Gladie? The one in the picture? Underwear girl?"

I shut my eyes in humiliation. Months before, I had gotten stuck upside down on a telephone pole, and half of the town saw my underpants. I would never live it down.

"You're famous," Bridget told me, biting into another gummy worm. "I'm feeling a lot better. Maybe I don't need the TUMS."

"I'm feeling a little nauseated, now," I said, opening the bottle and throwing two pills into my mouth.

"She's doing it, again. Stealing," the cashier whispered to Margie and Remington.

"I'm going to pay," I insisted. I dragged Bridget to the front and slapped the TUMS down on the counter. "This and four packages of deep-fried gummy worms."

"Six," Bridget corrected with her mouth full.

"Six," I said and took my wallet out of my purse. "I don't seem to have any cash," I said, searching through it. There was only a coupon for two-for-one chili cheese dogs at the pharmacy. Not a dollar to be seen.

"We take debit and credit," the cashier said.

A curtain of heat covered my face. I was out of cash in my bank account, too, and I was persona non-grata with all of the major credit card companies. With all of my organizing and hiding, I hadn't had any paying matches for a while.

"The thing is…" I started.

"Here you go," Bridget said, throwing a wad of cash onto the counter. "And toss me an Ultra-Kong sized slushy.

Do you have corn-nuts?"

"The slushy machine is self-serve," he told her.

"Didn't Dr. Sara say something about kale?" I asked her. She was going bonkers in the junk food department, even though she had spent the past few months creating the perfect baby with every organic superfood and supplement she could find.

"Gladie, there's no such thing as a kale slushy. Am I right?" she asked the cashier.

"We've got blue raspberry and Coke. We used to have Mountain Dew, but there was an incident."

"Damn it. I love Mountain Dew," Bridget said, kicking the floor. She waddled over to the slushy machine.

Margie was staring at me, and I wiped at my nose, in case something was hanging off it.

"Hey, Gladie, you didn't steal bubble gum, did you, babe?" Remington asked.

"No!" I said, finally able to tell the truth. I didn't steal the bubble gum. Sure, I had aided and abetted the theft of bubble gum, but I didn't actually steal it myself. Phew.

"She says she didn't steal the bubble gum," Remington said, his voice loud and booming. He towered over the cashier and had about fifty pounds on him. The cashier was visibly frightened of him.

"Fine," he said, throwing up his hands. "She didn't steal the bubble gum."

I smiled. It was a successful trip to the convenience store. No broken bones, I didn't have to go to the hospital, and I wasn't going to get arrested. "So funny that you thought I would steal bubble gum," I said, laughing. "Me. Stealing bubble gum. Me. So funny! Have you ever heard anything so funny? Bubble gum? I mean, if I was going to steal something, it wouldn't be bubble gum. Bubble gum!" I laughed loudly.

"Does that camera work?" Margie asked the cashier, pointing at a camera, which was hanging from the ceiling over his head.

"I think so. There are two more and one in the stockroom," he answered.

I gasped and wished for a stroke.

"This is great," Margie said, brightly. "We can get this worked out fast and nab the bubble gum bandits." She flashed me a look when she mentioned the bandits but looked away quickly. Good manners. I liked her, even though she was about to arrest me.

Unfortunately, it turned out that all of the video cameras worked, and after a call to the store's owner, the footage was hooked up to a laptop, and presto chango, there I was on the video screen, talking to the three bubble gum bandits.

"It's not what it looks like," I said.

"It looks like you're talking to three teenagers," Margie said.

"Then, it's exactly what it looks like."

"You look great, Gladie," Bridget said, sipping her Ultra-Kong sized slushy. "Usually the camera puts on twenty pounds."

"Thanks, Bridget." I did look good at that angle, filmed from up high. But then the footage showed me walk with the bandits into the stockroom, and it didn't matter how thin I looked.

"Why did you go in there with them?" Margie asked me.

"I was trying to be helpful. I didn't know they were bandits. It wasn't like I was aiding and abetting."

The footage showed me on one of the teenager's shoulders, tossing down boxes of bubble gum. "Okay, I might have been aiding and abetting, but it wasn't voluntary. It was involuntary aiding and abetting. Aiding and abetting against my will."

"You were being helpful," Margie supplied, understanding. I nodded, relieved. "Too bad you were being helpful to thieves."

"Gladie's a non-denominational helper," Remington said, winking at me.

The video continued with me falling dramatically onto the cashier's head, and the bandits running away. "See that? I'm a victim," I said. "I'm a victim of the bubble gum bandits. I've been bubble-gummed."

"She was framed," Bridget said, slurping her drink. "It's obvious. What is this? A kangaroo court?"

"What she said," I said.

"No one's on trial here, babe," Remington said. "Everything's cool. You were playing the duped side and didn't know it."

Huh?

"At least your pants stayed on this time," Margie said, patting me on the back.

Bridget slurped the last of her slushy. "That's true!" she announced. "You stayed totally dressed. That's really good, Gladie."

There's nothing better in this world than a best friend.

"No DICK," Remington said, looking at the screen. "The Chief isn't going to like this."

"They yelled something about no dick," I said. "Maybe they're feminists?"

"Feminists like dicks," Bridget insisted. "I'm a feminist, and I would kill for some dick. I'm a single woman, and I've been pregnant without dick for a thousand years. 'Responsible for your own orgasm,' my ass."

"I've never made it with a pregnant chick, but I'd make an exception for you," the cashier told Bridget.

We stared at the pimply faced young man with the greasy hair. Bridget pretended she hadn't heard him and dove back into her stash of gummy worms.

"Not that kind of dick," Remington said, finally. "DICK. Decency in Cannes Kids. It's an organization that has invaded the town after hearing about what happened with the Easter egg hunt."

"The dildos," I said, remembering. Ruth Fletcher, the octogenarian owner of the local tea shop had glued dildos onto the door of her competitor in a fit of rage.

"You were telling the truth?" Margie asked Remington.

He shrugged. "Cool never lies."

So, the bubble gum bandits were protesting a decency group, which was protesting our town. But why were the bandits protesting by stealing bubble gum? Bridget yawned. "I think I should go home. The last deep-fried gummy worm didn't land great."

"I have to take her home," I told Remington and Margie.

"You're not going to arrest her?" the cashier asked.

Remington shook his head. "Nope. We're going to release her back into the wild."

"It was nice meeting you," Margie told me and shook my hand. When I took my hand back, I double-checked my wrist for handcuffs. As hard as it was to believe, there was nothing there. I was free to go.

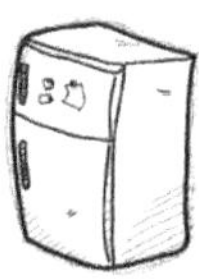

After taking Bridget to her house, I went home. Bird Gonzalez, the owner of the local beauty shop was there, giving my grandmother her rinse and set in the kitchen, while the pedicurist was going at Grandma's heels with a vengeance and working up a sweat. There was a spread on the table of a whole assortment of Mexican food. My stomach growled, and

I got a plate and sat down.

"This looks good," I said, scooping an enchilada onto my plate. "New place?" I asked my grandmother.

"No, Bird brought it."

"New diet?" I asked Bird.

She shook her head as she put a roller in my grandmother's hair. "I'm taking a break from diets."

I dropped my fork in surprise. "You're what?" Bird had gone from one diet to another ever since I had known her. She had drafted me into most of them, but they had all ended in failure for me. Since moving to Cannes, I had taken up my grandmother's bad eating habits, and I just couldn't seem to get back onto the healthy train.

"My nutritionist says I have diet fatigue," Bird explained.

"I think I have that, too," I said, taking a bite of the enchilada.

"She says that my body doesn't know which way's up. It's confusing carbs with protein. I'm all out of whack. So, I'm taking a break. If I can't fit into my pants, though, I'm going to kill that nutritionist." She waved a comb in my direction to highlight her point.

"I don't blame you," I said, tugging at my waistband. It was tight. I scooped another enchilada onto my plate.

"You better take it easy with that," Bird warned me. "You've got a wedding dress to fit into next month."

"I'm not having a big wedding," I said, but of course, that wasn't true. If only half of Grandma's friends came, there would be most of the town showing up to my wedding.

"Well, you can't go naked, can you? Definitely not after eating enchiladas."

She had a point. I was supposed to be on a bride diet. I was supposed to be eating broccoli and drinking protein shakes. I was supposed to be getting body hair removed, too. I probably needed fake eyelashes.

I was coming around to the idea of spending my entire life with Spencer, but why did we have to have a party where I was the center of attention?

"Gladie already has a wedding dress, and it fits her perfectly, no matter how many enchiladas she eats," my grandmother announced.

"I do?" I asked.

"Yes. It's my grandmother's dress. It's been perfectly preserved and you'll be gorgeous in it. She liked enchiladas, too."

If my grandmother said it was true, then it was true. She had a way of knowing things that couldn't be known, and a wise person never doubted her. I felt a wave of relief. Spencer was always beautifully dressed in Armani, so I knew he would be kicking it at the wedding. Now, with me wearing an antique wedding dress, he wouldn't show me up.

"The flowers and music are arranged, too," Grandma explained. "We only have one problem."

"Not the hair and makeup," Bird said, finishing rolling my grandmother's hair. "I'm taking care of that. You're going to look like a Grecian goddess."

That sounded good. Grecian goddesses had good hair and long eyelashes.

"What problem?" I asked Grandma, even though I didn't want to know because the whole idea of a wedding was giving me hives.

"The mayor wants to do the service," she sighed.

We all moaned in unison. The mayor was the dumbest man alive, who couldn't string two sentences together.

"I wish I could get you Mayor Fletcher, who did your parents' wedding," she continued. "He was a poet, but he's dead."

I flinched, as I remembered the box in the attic. It had my father's name on it. My grandmother couldn't have known it was there, or she would have opened it long ago. I didn't want to get her hopes up or upset her, so I decided to keep it a secret for the moment until I knew more. Maybe there was nothing of his in the box, anyway.

"That was delicious, Bird. Thank you," I said, washing my plate in the sink.

"It's your once in a lifetime chance at eating my enchiladas. As soon as my body stops being fatigued, I've got my eye on a diet meal prep delivery company."

I took the stairs two at a time to the attic. The box was still on the folding table, waiting for me. For some reason, I peeked out of the window, as if I was worried that Spencer would know what I was doing. Not that I was doing anything wrong, although it did feel like I was invading my father's privacy.

My father. I hadn't had a lot of time with him in my life, and I didn't know much about him. My memories of him were few and far between. I remembered one afternoon when he let me ride on his motorcycle with him. Grandma hated his motorcycle and made him promise that he would never allow me on it. But on that beautiful summer day, he broke his promise and treated me to a beautiful and perfect ride along the mountain roads with a stop at the end for Rocky Road ice cream. I closed my eyes and tried to recall what we talked about, but all I could remember was his wide smile and twinkling eyes and the way he looked at me as if he really liked me. Loved me.

It was just like how Spencer looked at me, but without the obvious picturing me naked thing that Spencer did more often than not.

I peeked through the attic window at the house across the street. The workers were sitting on the front lawn, eating their lunch. Spencer was nowhere to be seen, and I figured he had gone to work at the police station.

With a deep breath to gather my courage, I sat at the table and opened the box. "There's probably nothing in here," I told myself to stem my hopes. But I was wrong. The box was full of my father.

On top was a framed photo of him with my mother when they were very young. They were standing by a tree, and his arms were around her. Happy. I put the picture down on the table and dove into the box, again. I came out with a handful of report cards. I opened one from Cannes High School.

Math: D-. History: F. Physical Education: C. Biology: D-. French: F. English: A+.

It was like reading my own report cards except for the A in English. *Jonathan is a very popular student, and he spends most of his time socializing instead of paying attention in class. It's a shame that he's wasting his potential,* one of the teachers commented. Yep, it sounded familiar.

I put the report cards down next to the picture and pulled out some paper from the box. "Unpaid traffic tickets. Geez, Dad, you were worse than me," I said out loud. There were seven tickets, five for speeding and two for running stop signs. One of them caught my eye because it was dated on the last day of his life. "Going seventy in a thirty-five mile zone," I read. For the first time since he died, I wondered if he deserved to have a fatal accident. He was obviously reckless and thumbed his nose at authority. But to have gotten a speeding ticket the day of his accident was too much to bear. Didn't he care that his death would destroy the lives of the ones he loved? His family was never the same, again after his death, and he seemed to have tossed away his life without a second thought.

I put the tickets aside and dug deep into the box, taking out a handful of notebooks. I recognized them, immediately. They were my father's poems, the building blocks that eventually became his three published works. His handwriting was dreadful, but I managed to make out most of it.

One of the notebooks was different. It wasn't poetry, but rather some kind of journal. Short notes, doodles, and lists were scribbled all through it. Then, in my father's usual chicken scratch, there was a story about "Fart Boy," a cute children's story about an outcast boy.

A tear fell down my cheek, and I wiped it away. The story was proof of the potential my father had had and lost to a horrible accident. If he had lived, he might have had a new career writing for children.

Maybe, I thought, he was writing *Fart Boy* for his daughter.

Flipping through the notebook, I came to the last page. There were a series of three bullet-pointed notes that he had written.

Motorcycle accident.

Injuries too great to identify the body.

Man runs away to a new life, leaving his family behind.

I read through the notes twice to make sure that I had read them right. They weren't poetry. They weren't more children's fiction. They were notes for a plan. A horrible plan.

I saw stars, and the room spun around. The notebook fell from my fingers to the floor, and I gripped the table for support and to hold on to consciousness. It felt like I had been hit in the gut. I was faced with a reality that I had never contemplated in my wildest imagination. Not even when I was a lonely little girl missing my father and praying to God to make him return.

But here was the truth in black and white.
My father had faked his death.
My father was alive.

CHAPTER 3

A little lie never hurt anybody, dolly. And there's a lot of lies in love. Sure, there's a lot of truth, too, but a lot of lies, as well. As a matchmaker, you're going to have to navigate the lies and figure out which you're going to let fly and which you're going to nip in the bud. Weigh the lies and figure out which ones do some good and which ones don't. Remember that the matchmaker's first rule is: "Do no harm, unless you need to." Or some fakakta thing like that.

Lesson 123, Matchmaking advice from your
Grandma Zelda

I needed to tell my grandmother that her son was really alive.

I couldn't tell my grandmother that her son was really alive until I knew for sure.

But she would want to know.

But she would be hurt if it wound up not being true.

No way could I keep this secret.

I had to keep this secret.

I realized that I was standing up and spinning around like a top each time I had an opposing thought. I was my own presidential debate, debating both sides of the issue.

As much as I wanted to run around the house, screaming, "my father's alive!", I forced myself to be patient. I would have to find out for sure if my father was alive or dead before I said a word to my grandmother. There was no way I was going to traumatize her, and that's exactly what I would do if I said something, gave her hope, and it turned out that he was dead. So, I had to be patient until I got to the bottom of things.

Unfortunately, patience wasn't my strong suit.

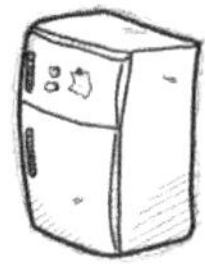

It took four hours for me to discover that everything about my life was a lie. By the time I returned downstairs, Spencer had returned and was in the kitchen, drinking orange juice out of the jug. He wiped his mouth with the back of his hand when he saw me and arched an eyebrow in a gesture so predatory that I looked down to make sure I wasn't naked.

"There you are," he said, putting the orange juice back in the fridge. "Call me crazy, but I was starting to think you were hiding from me."

"Crazy," I said and looked at my shoes. "Why would I hide from you? I love you and am going to marry you."

I looked up to see him smirk his little smirk. "Just because we're getting married doesn't mean we have to stop doing the one-eyed monkey."

"What's the one-eyed monkey?"

He approached me, his eyes never leaving mine, his smirk planted on his face, like a neon sign announcing his virility and determination. Slowly, he slipped his arms around me and pulled me in close. His cologne was intoxicating, spinning me into a cloud of desire. Spencer was in amazing shape, hard and muscular and big like the man of young girls' fantasies. And old women's fantasies, too, I would have bet money on it.

He walked forward, pushing me back until I was against the kitchen wall. One of his hands moved to the place on the wall above my head, and his other hand touched me on my hoochie mama over my pants. It was like I was Kansas in 1880, and he was staking his homestead claim.

I was totally ready to let him settle in and build on me.

The thing he was doing with his eyes, the look that lasered into my brain and down through my body into my humming pelvis, was now over. Instead, he was focused on my neck, trailing light kisses from my collar bone, up to my ear.

I shuddered. My insides were hot, molten lava, turning my organs into mush, and I wondered vaguely if my spleen would work after Spencer was done with me in my grandmother's kitchen.

And I also wondered what a spleen did.

Who cared? I was being thoroughly seduced by a man who had written the encyclopedia of seduction from A to Z, and he also knew a ton about anatomy. So, anything besides the here and now was totally uninteresting to me.

"While you've been hiding, I've been planning," he breathed into my ear, his hot breath ironically sending shivers through me. He wasn't totally unaffected, either. His hard body was getting harder by the second, a screaming siren that Spencer was raring to go, and I was the one he was raring to go with.

"A new couch? Wallpaper?"

"No. But we're going couch shopping this week. I'm talking about another kind of planning. What I'm going to do with you." He punctuated his statement with a gentle bite on my earlobe.

"Oh," I sighed. "What are you going to do with me?" I asked because I really wanted to know, even though more than a small part of me wanted him to throw me onto the kitchen table and screw me like a light bulb, even if my grandmother was somewhere in the house and could walk in at any moment.

"I was thinking that there's a place up in the mountains where they break away and there's a large meadow with thick, lush grass. I'm going to take you there at sunset on a warm evening," he breathed into my ear. "And as the stars fill the sky, I'm going to lay you down in that lush grass and strip you naked slowly."

He paused dramatically. I slapped his back. "Then what?" I urged. "What happens when I'm naked in the grass? Will you be naked, too?"

His hand worked its magic lower down, while he leaned in, his mouth touching my ear. "Naked. Ready. Focused on giving you pleasure."

"That's a good thing to focus on," I breathed, my eyes closed, and my body squirming against him. With each word, he was driving me closer to a drooling mass of hormones, two inches from a rockin' orgasm.

"I'll glide my hands down the inside of your thighs, separating your legs," he continued. "Finally, thankfully, I'll touch you here." Spencer's fingers pressed between my legs to illustrate exactly where he would touch me. "And find that spot that makes you purr like a kitten."

"A kitten? I purr like a kitten?"

"Yes. You purr like a pussy. So, I'll lean over you, gripping your ass in my hands and lifting you to my mouth. To my tongue."

Yowza. Spencer did words really good. And words were the worst things he did. He did other things really, really, really good. I started to drool, thinking about those things.

My leg raised and wrapped around his hip, as if by magic, like I was Pinocchio with strings, and Spencer was pulling them. I was torn between wanting to hear the rest of his plans for me and wanting to beg him to take me upstairs and ravage me like a romance novel from the 1980s.

But it turned out I didn't get either of my choices because this was my grandmother's house, and even in its quietest moments, it was Grand Central.

"We're coming in, dolly," Grandma announced from the hallway. "Have to do it now before you get naked."

"You were about to get naked?" Spencer asked me, like he was the one-million-and-one person to shop at a store, one person too late for the million-shopper grand prize.

"Oh, yeah," I told him. "Very naked."

His face dropped in obvious disappointment, and he stepped back away from me, adjusting his designer tie, and straightening his designer suit. I had just enough time to wipe the drool from my chin before my grandmother walked into the kitchen with a couple people following her, carrying bakery boxes.

"Cake tasting," Grandma announced.

"Cake tasting," I breathed, watching them put the boxes down on the table. It was the only good thing about having a wedding, as far as I could tell, and it was the only thing that could compete with getting naked with Spencer.

"Hello," one of the women said. She was a tiny little old lady, wearing a pink smock, and she sounded like Minnie Mouse when she spoke. "I'm Sandy, your nuptial sugar specialist from Cannes Cakes. I'm honored to be part of your happily ever after celebration."

She took my hand in hers, and she shed real tears,

making me uncomfortable. I hadn't shed any tears about my happily ever after celebration.

"Sandy is the best cake baker in the southwest," Grandma told me. "She's a miracle worker with Heath bars and milk chocolate."

"That sounds really good, doesn't it?" I asked Spencer. He tried to drum up his usual smirk, but he was still wearing his I've-been-cockblocked face.

Sandy and her assistant opened the cake boxes and arranged seven beautiful, little round cakes on my grandmother's table. I drooled even more than I did when Spencer talked dirty to me. I slumped onto a chair, and Spencer got us plates.

Grandma, Spencer, and I went through the seven cakes, tasting each one and then tasting them again. And again. I loved all of them except for the one with raspberry. Why did people insist on putting fruit in sweets? There's no place for that kind of insanity in this world.

"I like cake number five best, but number two is a close second," Spencer said, licking the frosting from his fork.

"Two is raspberry," I told Spencer, nonplussed. "You didn't taste the raspberry?"

"Okay, number five," he said.

Number five was good, but I didn't want to miss out on one, three, four, six, and seven. "Can we have more than one cake?" I asked, taking the last bite of number six.

"That sounds like a good idea," Grandma said with her mouth full of number three.

Sandy smiled wide. "I'm so glad you said that! We can do a seven-layer cake, each layer a different cake."

"Perfect," I said, overjoyed. "Except for the raspberry."

"Except for the raspberry," she agreed.

"This was fun. Thank you," I told my grandmother and gave her a hug.

"All of this cake was a wonderful appetizer. I'll order us some ribs and macaroni and cheese for dessert," she said.

Spencer cleared the dishes and gave her a kiss on her head. "You're the best, Zelda," he said.

After dinner, Spencer and I went upstairs. I had almost forgotten about my father during the cake tasting, but it all came flooding back to me during the ribs. I was so worried that I was going to spill the beans at the table that I kept feeding my face. Rib after rib went into my mouth, so that the words wouldn't escape. As soon as possible, I was going to have to find the truth out about my father, or there was no way I could hold back from telling my grandmother that I believed my father had faked his death.

Spencer kept his hand on my lower back while we walked upstairs. The secret was too much for me to keep. I couldn't keep my mouth shut any longer, and there weren't any more ribs to stuff in them. Grandma was finally out of earshot, and I couldn't wait to tell Spencer about my father.

"You know," I started.

"Yes," he said, as we reached the second floor. "I know. I feel it, too. If I had known that commitment and monogamy were so powerful, I would have gotten married years ago."

"You didn't know me years ago."

"What's your point, Pinky?"

"I'm going to let that slide."

"Seriously, I'm pretty overwhelmed with the house and the wedding, and the reality that we're going to be together forever. Overwhelmed in a good way," he pointed out, as we walked into my bedroom. He pulled me in close and rested his forehead on mine. "And I wanted to let you know how happy I am that the house and the wedding are now your number one priority. No murder investigations. No wreaking havoc on the town or sticking your nose in with the DICK nightmare. No tilting at windmills. Just focusing on us. Thank you, Pinky. It means a lot to me. I love you."

Shit.

He was so earnest and romantic that I didn't have the heart to tell him about my father, that I had another windmill to tilt at, and that I was literally hunting for a ghost. I didn't want to let Spencer down. So, I would have to keep my father thing to myself, find out the truth, and then tell Spencer afterward, all the while pretending to prioritize couch shopping and flower girl dresses.

Being in a committed relationship was a minefield.

THE BIG KILL

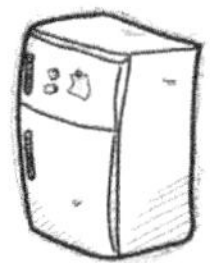

After Spencer and I romped in the hay for two hours and then romped in the shower, he fell dead asleep, and I snuck out of bed to call Lucy.

She picked up on the first ring, and I told her about my plan to get to the bottom of my father's so-called death. She was totally on board.

"The cock crows at midnight," she whispered into the phone when I was done telling her the plan. "Roger, over and out. Second star to the right and straight on 'til morning."

I didn't sleep a wink. About an hour before sunrise, I rolled out of bed and landed with a soft thud onto the floor. From there, I crawled out of the room and shut the door with a click. I had stashed my clothes in the hallway when Spencer had fallen asleep...black yoga pants, a black sweatshirt, and white Keds because I didn't have black sneakers.

Miraculously, I managed to drive away without waking my grandmother or Spencer. Lucy was waiting for me on the sidewalk outside of her new house, which looked a lot like Hearst Castle. Lucy was wearing black, too. I stopped the car, and she opened the door, slipping into the front seat and dragging a large shovel in with her.

"What's the shovel for?" I asked.

"You know," she said, breathlessly.

I took a good, hard look at the shovel. "We're not

going to do you know," I insisted.

"It's a good shovel. I got it at Neiman Marcus."

"What do you think we're doing?" I asked, even though I already knew what she thought.

"We're going to prove that your daddy isn't dead, darlin'."

"Yes, that true, but we're not going to use a shovel."

Lucy adjusted her black ski cap on her head. "Then, how are we going to dig him up? You have a machine? Did you bribe a couple gravediggers? Clever, Gladie! Very clever."

"Lucy, we're not going to dig up my father. It's my father. I'm already traumatized enough from finding dead people who were total strangers. I'm not going to come face to face with a dead person who's my father."

Lucy seemed to think about that for a moment and then nodded her head. "That's understandable."

"We're going to break into the records' room at the police department and get a DNA sample that way. There should be a box of his bloody clothes, there," I explained.

"Oh, that's smart." She dumped the shovel onto the backseat. "By the way, Bridget said she wanted to come with us. So, pick her up on the way."

I found Bridget standing on the sidewalk in front of her townhouse. She was wearing a dark muumuu, and she was doing some kind of dance. I stopped the car in front of her, and she got in.

"Thank goodness you called, Lucy," Bridget said. "The nights are the worst. I can't wait until I have the baby, and I can finally get some sleep."

I put the car into drive and drove off toward the Historic District. "What were you doing on the sidewalk?" I asked Bridget.

"Zumba. I heard it was good for starting labor. I still have the farting labor, but the real labor is eluding me." As proof, she farted. "I'm a monster. I fart. I have hemorrhoids. My feet have grown two sizes. I don't buy into gender normative stereotypes of women being dainty little females, but...but...but...I want to be pretty."

She sniffed and started to weep but stopped after a couple seconds. "Tea Time is open," she announced, excitedly, hopping up and down in her seat and pointing as we drove near the tea shop. "Let's get me some coffee."

"Aren't pregnant women supposed to stay away from coffee, darlin'?" Lucy asked.

"I don't give a shit. I haven't had caffeine in months, and maybe it'll jolt the baby out of my pelvis."

I didn't want to stop. It was almost sunrise and the chances of getting caught would increase with daylight, but I hadn't slept all night, and I could go for a free latte before I committed a felony. I made a U-turn and parked in front of Tea Time. I noticed that there was a large DICK poster glued onto every lamppost along Main Street.

We walked into Tea Time, and we were the only customers in the shop. Tea Time used to be a saloon in the late 1800s when Cannes was founded after gold was discovered. There were still a couple of bullet holes in the wall from its Wild West days and the original bar, which was meticulously kept in pristine condition by the owner, an ornery octogenarian named Ruth Fletcher, who loved all things tea and hated all coffee drinkers. I had done a favor for Ruth a few months before, and she awarded me with a car and free lattes for a year.

Ruth's customer service left a lot to be desired, but she made a kickass latte.

"Not you, again. I'm done taking your shit!" Ruth hollered as we entered. She wielded a broom over her head, like she was starring in a *300* remake, cast entirely of geriatric women in sensible shoes.

She took two steps forward and stopped, squinting at us. "Oh, it's you," she said. "I thought you were DICK, again."

There were so many comebacks, I didn't know where to start.

"Don't get me started on those DICK people," Lucy complained. "Who are they to lecture me on decency?"

There was an awkward silence. We had recently found out that Lucy had been a high-priced call girl before she got married a few months before.

"Well, you know what I mean," Lucy added after a moment.

"What's going on with this DICK thing?" I asked. "I haven't been around. I haven't gotten the full rundown."

"Ruth, I need a coffee," Bridget interrupted. "Full octane. And give me three chocolate chip scones. On the double, Ruth. I'm not joking. I'm bearing life."

"Big deal," Ruth spat at Bridget. "I slept with FDR. When you sleep with FDR, then you can talk to me about bearing life."

"I've grown a human being in my belly!" Bridget yelled, stomping her feet.

"Okay, okay," I said, stepping in between them. "This is getting ugly. Can't we just be friends? Don't let DICK bring you down to their level."

"Fine," Ruth grumbled. "I guess I've been in a bad mood. I've had too much DICK. DICK won't leave me alone. They're in here all the time since they showed up in town. If they think I give a shit about decency, they've got another thing comin'. Decency hasn't been alive and well in this country since my Aunt Fanny was in diapers. They want me to rat out kids who're turning left when they should be turning right. You know what I told them?"

"I have an idea," I mumbled.

"I told them to stick it where the sun don't shine."

"Did you mention that you were the one who stuck the dildos onto the doors next door, so you're responsible for them invading Cannes to clean up our filthy town?" I asked Ruth.

"Don't poke the bear, Gladie," Ruth growled.

"I'll take that as a no."

Bridget took the entire platter of scones off the bar and put it on a table, where we sat down. We ordered coffee, much to Ruth's annoyance. I watched Ruth make our coffee, and it dawned on me that she knew my father and had been around when he had had his accident.

"I'll get the coffee," I told Lucy and Bridget, and walked up to Ruth at the bar.

"It's not ready, yet," Ruth grumbled.

"That's fine." I drew an invisible circle on the counter with my finger and avoided eye contact with her at all costs. "So, you were there when my father had his accident, right?"

Ruth's head snapped up in my direction. "Where did that question come from?"

"Nowhere. Just curious."

"I've never spoken about that day." We locked eyes, and I saw tears in hers. I had never seen Ruth cry before. I didn't even know her tear ducts still worked. My chest got tight, as if there was a little man inside, squeezing it hard.

Guilt. Sympathy. I knew it well. I would have to do without her first-hand account.

"Sorry, Ruth," I said, took the coffee, and walked back to our table.

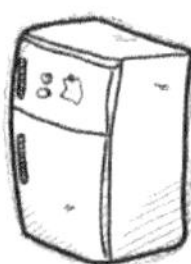

"I feel great!" Bridget announced, hopping up and down in the backseat after our trip to Tea Time. "I don't know why I have so much energy!"

"Maybe because she had three cups of coffee after six months of no caffeine," Lucy said to me out of the corner of her mouth.

"So, where're we going?" Bridget asked, still hopping up and down.

"Records room," I answered. "Sun's coming up. We'll have to hide the car a couple blocks away. We've been training our whole lives for this, ladies. Don't let me down."

We drove through the quiet town to the police station. As far as I knew, there really wasn't any way to break into the records room. We were going to have to finesse our way in, which was breaking in through lying instead of physical force.

Luckily, Sergeant Fred Lytton had the night shift and was still around for another hour when we showed up, and Fred liked me. I texted him from the back door, where we stood in our black outfits, and I was waiting for him with a large to-go cup filled with hot chocolate and a bag filled with a half dozen rum balls from Tea Time.

The door opened, and Fred gave me a big smile. "Underwear Girl," he breathed, like I was Princess Grace or some other angelic beauty.

"Hi, Fred. We've brought you a morning treat."

"Oh look at that. You brought me a present. I forgot to get you something. Oh, wait a minute." He riffled through his pants pocket and pulled out a cellophane-wrapped gumball. "Grape gum. You want?"

"Sure," I said, taking it.

"Got any more?" Bridget asked, hopping up and down on her heels. The caffeine was working on her like a trip to the bathroom at Studio 54 in 1982.

"That was my last one," Fred told her. "It was a twelve-gumball night."

I handed Bridget my gum. "Here. For the baby," I said. "Hey, Fred," I continued, giving him all of my attention and possibly batting my eyelids and flipping my hair. "I'm taking the girls on a small tour of the station. All right?"

"Sure, whatever the Chief says, I do."

I felt terrible lying to Fred. Spencer definitely didn't say I could take my friends on a tour of the police station before sunrise, and there was no way he would let us run free in the records room. I crossed my fingers behind my back.

"Yep," I told Fred, looking up at the ceiling.

He turned sideways and let us enter. "Smooth as my grandmother's chocolate puddin'," Lucy whispered in my ear as we walked inside. "After this, you might think about robbing banks."

CHAPTER 4

High Hopes. That's a song, bubbeleh. It's about high hopes. Your matches will have high hopes, and sometimes you'll have to tamper down those high hopes to a low or middle hope and sometimes you'll have to boost those high hopes to over-the-top high hopes. You understand, dolly? One match might need high hopes in order to muster the enthusiasm required to be a good date. Another match might need lower hopes so that they're not disappointed when even Clark Gable walks in the room and tells them he loves them. Hope is subjective. Hope varies from one person to another. At least I hope it does.

Lesson 39, Matchmaking advice from your Grandma Zelda

Fred was delighted to be our tour guide, and no matter how I wracked my brain, I couldn't figure out how to ditch him and get us down to the records room in order to steal my father's clothing, so that we could do a DNA test.

"This is my desk," Fred explained, running his palm over it. "I stand here and talk to people and do paperwork. The place would go down if it weren't for me at this desk."

"Very interesting, darlin'," Lucy said. "Where's the records room?"

I elbowed her in her side, and she *oophed* loudly.

"Downstairs," he explained. "We don't normally go there during a tour."

"But this is a VIP tour, darlin'," Lucy said, like she was at Neiman Marcus, turning her nose up at an off-the-rack collection.

Fred rubbed his chin, and I could practically see the cogs of his brain spinning. He was stuck between wanting to please me and not wanting Spencer to go down on him hard. I felt the familiar wave of guilt again. I didn't want to get him into trouble, but there was no stopping me from finding out the truth about my father. So, I was about to tell him a big whopper in order to get us down there when Bridget saved me from myself.

"I have to pee," she said, her voice sounding like a villain from a comic book movie. "Now. Pee. Now!"

"Down the hall," Fred squeaked, pointing.

Bridget grabbed his arm. "Take me there," she ordered.

The minute they were gone, Lucy and I jumped into action, making a beeline for the stairwell. "I feel like Kiefer Sutherland, and I'm going to save the world in twenty-four hours, or in this case the three minutes it takes Bridget to pee," she said, as we rushed downstairs.

I opened the door to the basement, and we were greeted by a chain-link fence, and behind it was a giant area of shelves filled with boxes. "It's like *Raiders of the Lost Ark*," I breathed, pulling out my lock pick set from my purse. I couldn't sew or cook, but I had taken to lock picking with amazing skill and speed. The padlock to the chain-link fence opened easily, and we walked inside.

"Where on earth do we start?" Lucy asked.

"Let's look under B for Burger."

But it didn't take us long to discover that the boxes were organized numerically and not alphabetically. "We could hack the computer system," Lucy suggested. "If we knew anything about computers."

We looked at the computer on a small table by the chain-link fence. "Do you know how to turn it on?" I asked Lucy.

"There should be a button."

We couldn't find a button, so it was reasonably certain we wouldn't be able to hack the system to find where my father's case box was. "Let's do this old school," I suggested. "If it's numerical, then it should be by date. Let's go backward and find it that way."

It was a dumb plan. There were a gazillion boxes. I had more of a chance of finding the actual Lost Ark than finding my father's box. But Lucy was game to search through the private, confidential boxes, so we went back five aisles and opened a random box.

"Sam Dervish, September 2000," Lucy read from a file inside a box. "Oh my God. I think his toe is in this box. Do you want to see his toe?"

"I'm pretty sure I don't want to see his toe."

Reluctantly, she closed the box, and we moved on. "Who would have thought you could lose a toe, making a smoothie?" Lucy wondered aloud, as we searched through boxes. "I never trusted those smoothie people. Why would you turn food into a drink when there are perfectly good drinks? Oh, speaking of lunch and drinks, let's have Mexican for lunch today with margaritas. With lots of salt. Yum."

It was good that Lucy's appetite wasn't affected by the toe. I had to admit that margaritas sounded good to me, too, even though my stomach was roiling as we got closer to 1992, the year my father died.

"I might have to pee, again," I heard Bridget say by the entrance to the records room. They had come back. Lucy and I froze, throwing our bodies against the boxes, as if we could hide that way.

"Do you have two bladders?" I heard Fred ask Bridget.

"Of course I don't. I have one bladder, and one baby sitting on it. It's not easy creating life, you know. I'm making a person from scratch inside my body."

"Maybe it's the baby's bladder. That would make two," Fred suggested. "Your bladder and its bladder, you know."

"It doesn't work that way, Fred. I have one bladder. One."

"I knew a woman with two bladders," he continued, not letting go of his theory for her robust pee-pee activity. "The doctor offered to take one out, but she kept both of them."

"I have one bladder," she insisted, her pregnant voice raspy and full of rage.

"But I guess with two bladders maybe you wouldn't have to pee as much because you could hold twice as much. I don't know how it works with two bladders."

There was a long pause before Bridget spoke, again. "Yep, I have to pee, again. Come on."

I heard the gate open and close. Thank goodness for Bridget's bladder. It was the perfect diversion. As soon as they left, Lucy and I got back to it, feverishly ripping open boxes because we didn't have a lot of time before Fred would return and we would be found out.

Lucy opened a box, looked inside for a second and slammed it shut. "Darlin', I found it," she said and touched my arm.

I stumbled backward a step and clutched at my chest. My heart was beating like the Marines Band, and it felt like it was going to explode. "Wait," I said. "Wait. Wait. Wait."

"You want me to leave so that you can look at it alone?" Lucy asked.

"Yes. No. Yes. No." I took a deep breath and tried, again. "Yes. No. Yes. No."

"Gladie, I think you're broken. Should I slap you to jumpstart your brain?"

I probably needed to be slapped. Lucy was right. I was broken. But I didn't want to be slapped. Faced with a box that represented my father's death, I couldn't move myself to look inside. His life was one thing, but his death was something different altogether.

"You want me to do it?" Lucy asked me, as if she was reading my mind.

"Yes. No. Yes. No."

"I'm good at slapping. Let me slap you."

"No. I'm going to do it." As much as I didn't want to examine my father's death, I didn't want someone else to be the first to look into it. I wasn't the most private person in the world, but where my father was concerned, I was Fort Knox.

I took the box from Lucy and sat down on the floor. She sat across from me, and I put the box down between us. I stared at the lid.

"Remember why you're doing this," Lucy said. "Your father might still be alive. So this might not be his box. It might be someone else's box."

We locked eyes. I hadn't thought about that, about who the someone else could be. And if my father faked his death, then where did he get this someone else who died instead of him? I squirmed a little. "Maybe it's not such a good idea to be poking my nose in," I said.

"You may be right, darlin', but when has that ever stopped you before?"

"This might get complicated. Messy."

"Again, when has that ever stopped you before?"

She had a point. No matter how messy or complicated, nothing was going to stop me from snooping in the box and getting to the bottom of my father's death. Or his not death.

I opened the box.

The sound of the fence's gate opening broke through the silence, and I heard the familiar clack-clack of expensive Italian men's shoes on the cement floor. Uh oh.

"Quick," I whispered to Lucy. "I need a plausible excuse about why I'm sitting on the floor in the records room with my father's box."

"Insanity," she whispered back. "Drugs. Alien abduction. Leprosy."

"I like the alien abduction one. You think it'll work?"

"No. You might have luck with leprosy, though."

"Don't go in there," I heard Bridget shout. Best friends are the best. She was doing everything in her power to stop me from being found out.

"What's going on, Bridget?"

There it was, the voice that went with expensive Italian men's shoes. Spencer. The Chief of Police. My fiancé.

"I'm bearing life. I'm the earth goddess. I am woman."

"What does that have to do with the records room?" he asked her.

"This is going to be bad," Lucy whispered to me.

"You should have let me bring in the shovel. I could have beaned him in the head and he wouldn't have been the wiser."

"Damnit, Lucy. Why didn't I let you bring in the shovel?"

"I have a baby punching my bladder," I heard Bridget tell Spencer. Her voice was getting closer, and so were Spencer's Italian shoes. "Stop. Don't go any further. Help! Police brutality! Attica!"

"Bridget, I haven't touched you. Are you okay?"

"Rodney King! Rodney King!" she shouted.

"That's our cue," I whispered to Lucy. I grabbed the box, and we got up, tip-toeing as quietly as we could, as far away from Spencer as we could get.

It wasn't far.

"You know, this isn't working, Bridget. I could carry you for ten miles and not work up a sweat," I heard Spencer tell Bridget as they came closer.

"You could?" she asked him, obviously impressed.

"Without breathing hard," he said.

Then, we saw them. And they saw us. Bridget was holding onto Spencer and digging her feet into the floor, so that he was forced to drag her as he walked, but like he said, it wasn't hard for him. Spencer blinked and stopped in his tracks when he saw me, and his eyes went from me to the box I was holding and back again.

"It's not what it looks like," I said.

"It looks like you're stealing official records."

"Not stealing," Lucy said. "Not exactly stealing."

"I just… we just… you see… oh, damn it," I mumbled and then rocked back on my heels and ran in the opposite direction.

"Run, Gladie, run!" Bridget shouted.

"Are you kidding me?" Spencer griped and ran after me.

Of course, he was going to catch me sooner or later. I mean, we lived together, so it was inevitable. But I couldn't stop running.

He caught me in five seconds. He took me down like a linebacker, and my father's box flew out of my hands, the contents sailing through the air and landing here and there, scattered over the floor. Spencer blocked my fall, protecting my body as we landed. Cradling the back of my head with his big right hand, he looked into my eyes. I read confusion and tenderness in them. My Spencer was all things. Why did I run from him?

"Gladys Burger, what the fuck are you doing?" he demanded and let me drop.

"Don't call me Gladys."

He stood and smoothed out his suit and ran his fingers through his hair. "One minute we're cake tasting, and the next you're stealing official documents. Are you snooping again, Gladys?"

I sat up and tried to calm myself down. He knew that I hated to be called Gladys. "I'm not snooping. I'm not stealing. That box is mine. Sort of."

"Tell him about your daddy," Lucy said.

I swallowed. "I found something in the attic when I was organizing. I think my father faked his death."

I told him about the journal entry and my plan to test his DNA. Spencer helped me up and pulled me in close. "Why didn't you tell me, Pinky? I would have helped you."

"But my priorities are supposed to be with the house and the wedding," I said, my voice cracking.

Spencer tucked a strand of my hair behind my ear and glided his thumb over my bottom lip. "Oh, Pinky. Family comes first, especially this family. You should have come to me."

"But the bamboo floors. And the couch."

"Wow, I've been a royal jackass, haven't I?" He leaned forward and rested his forehead against mine. "I just wanted the right couch to lay you down on and make love to you."

"Oh," I breathed, my face getting hot.

"Let me handle this for you."

"Can you do it fast?"

"As fast as humanly possible," he said. "I can't believe you thought I wouldn't help you. It's not like you're chasing murderers and putting your life in jeopardy."

"No, it's not like that," I said and a shiver went up my spine. In an instant, a vision flashed before me of my father on his motorcycle, driving around a bend. A figure in shadow stepped forward.

Bridget moaned, and my vision vanished. "This was beautiful," she gushed. "I love to see true respect between the sexes who are in a relationship instead of the usual patriarchal, abusive dominance baloney that… that… ohhh…"

"What happened?" Lucy asked. "Her diatribe was cut off mid-sentence. That's never happened to her before."

Bridget clutched at her crotch. I had seen this before. Bridget moaned, again.

"Something's happening," she said. "Something… ahhh… ohhh… ow!"

"What's happening? What's happening?" Spencer demanded, his voice an octave higher than normal. Sweat had popped out on his upper lip, and he looked around him, as if he was searching for an escape route.

"The miracle of birth, I expect," Lucy said.

"Here? Now?" Spencer asked.

Bridget crouched down. "He's coming! He's coming! It's happening!"

CHAPTER 5

One day when I was a little girl, my mother told me that I had the gift for love and that I would be a matchmaker just like she was. Up until then I wanted to be an ice-skating veterinarian, but the moment the words came out of her mouth, I knew she was telling the truth. In fact, as she spoke, I had a vision that Uncle Herbert would be very happy with Tilly, who sold tamales door-to-door. Two days later, I asked Tilly to come inside, and she fed Uncle Herbert a tamale, and they were married for fifty years. Sometimes it happens like that, dolly. You just know and even though you had your heart set on doing a double-axel at night after a day of neutering dogs, you can try to kibbitz around, but in the end, you can't resist the calling. This is called following your truth, even if it's just a vision in your head that no one else can see.

Lesson 21, Matchmaking advice from your Grandma Zelda

He wasn't coming. It wasn't happening.

Again.

"Alexa, music off," Dr. Sara ordered in exam room one.

"Was it farting labor, again?" Bridget asked, dejected.

"Braxton Hicks," Dr. Sara explained. "That's good. Your body is practicing to give birth to your son." She smiled and clanged mini-cymbals over Bridget's baby. "There you go. You're one with the universe. I think the baby will be calm now until it's time."

She kept smiling, but her body was tense, and her left eyebrow was spasming. She had false labor PTSD. I recognized it. Bridget wasn't doing too well, either. When Dr. Sara left the room, Bridget broke down in tears.

"She hates me," Bridget blubbered.

I petted her head. "No she doesn't. Nobody could hate you, Bridget."

"She hates me because my damned uterus won't work right. This baby is wedged in me and refuses to come out."

"He'll come out when it's time," I said, trying to make her feel better.

Bridget grabbed a handful of my shirt and pulled me down to her. "Liar," she growled. "He's never coming out. Never. I'll be the first woman to be pregnant for six solid years. He'll get so big that he'll explode my belly, like in *Alien*. Alien, Gladie. My son is the Alien. That's not good, you know, Gladie. I might not have a lot of experience with babies, but I know enough to know that Alien babies are not the best kind of babies."

I stared at her belly, half-expecting an alien to burst from it. "I don't think you have an alien in there," I said, but I didn't sound totally convinced.

"I'll tell you this, Gladie. No more false labor for me. I don't care how much agony I'm in, I'm not calling Dr. Sara until my baby's head is halfway out of my vaginal canal. Okay?"

I didn't answer. I was visualizing a baby's head in her vaginal canal and thinking that that would hurt like a bitch and that I wouldn't want to be there when it happened.

With no baby on the way, Bridget and I decided to meet Lucy for lunch at Saladz. Spencer had already swabbed my cheek on our way out of the police station so that he could compare my DNA with the DNA found at the scene of my father's accident. Since my grandmother was handling my wedding, I found myself with nothing to do except be a lady who lunched. But I couldn't help but feel that my work wasn't done where my father was concerned and that I had stirred up something big.

"Gladie, what's wrong with your face?" Bridget asked me, as she ate her last bite of French toast and sauerkraut.

"What do you mean?" I asked, touching my face.

"I know that face," Lucy said, pointing her perfectly manicured finger at me. "It's the whodunit face. It's the Miss Marple face. It's the… what happened? Where did that face come from? Did I miss something?"

"No! No," I said, turning my traitorous face away from her. "It's just my father."

"Oh, that must be it," Lucy said. She was on her second margarita, and her speech was slightly slurred. Bridget's caffeine buzz was finally dying down, and she was yawning.

I took my friends home, but I wasn't ready to return to my grandmother's house just yet. Since we didn't have a movie theater, I went back to Tea Time. This time, business was booming, but Ruth was in a terrible mood. Maybe because she was on her knees, under a table.

I crouched down. "Hey, there, Ruth. Can I get a latte?"

She pointed a metal tool at me. "Can't you see I'm busy?"

"I thought you might be taking a break."

"I'm scraping bubble gum off the undersides of my tables, like the whole town is doing."

"Ruth, the whole town isn't scraping gum off your tables."

She crawled out from under the table and lifted her hand up. "Help me, dammit. My knees haven't seen cartilage in fifty years."

I pulled her up, and her knees cracked loudly. "You want me to call a doctor?"

"Why?" she demanded. "I'm not afraid of a little bone crunching. Didn't I already give you a latte today?"

"It's a two-latte day, today, Ruth."

She limped toward the bar. "You'd be a lot better off if you drank some tea, Gladie. Coffee is barbaric."

"You're so right," I said. "I'll drink tea at some point. Not today, though."

Strong arms wrapped around me, and I felt Spencer's body up against my back. "Came to talk to you," he whispered in my ear.

I turned around in his arms. "How did you know I was here?"

"I may have trackers on your car and your phone."

"That's a violation of privacy."

"No, that's called an ounce of prevention."

"You're here," I said, realizing. "That means you have the DNA results?"

"DNA tests take longer than two hours, Pinky. But I looked through the evidence box, and this is going to be hard to hear."

"Tell me," I breathed and clenched my fists to prepare myself for the worst. I didn't know what the worst could be. That my father faked his death? That my father didn't fake his death?

"I looked at the incident photos," Spencer explained. "They're your father. They match up with the photos of him in Zelda's house."

"But they said his injuries were too great for us to identify his body." My voice cracked, and I willed myself not to give into the emotion of losing a father that I had already lost years before.

"He was pretty beat up, obviously, and I figure they were trying to spare your mother and grandmother. But it's him. Would you like to see the photos? I'll give you free access to the evidence box whenever you want."

"You will?" I asked, surprised. Spencer had a long history of blocking me where dead people were concerned.

"I told you. This is family. It's not like you're bloodhounding, again."

"Right," I said, looking up at the ceiling.

Ruth slapped my latte cup on the bar. "Hey, cop, what are you doing about these bubble gum bandits?" she growled at Spencer. "I'm scraping gum off every surface. They sneak in here and stick it wherever they can."

Spencer put his serious cop face on. "We're working on it, Ruth. They outnumber us."

"They're going after DICK, which I wholeheartedly approve," she said. "But I have nothing to do with DICK. I don't even let DICK within my walls!"

Spencer smirked and slapped his hand over his mouth to cover it up. "Yes, Ruth. We're implementing a curfew for minors, starting tonight. That should help."

Ruth harrumphed loudly and scowled at Spencer. His phone rang, and he answered. "What do you mean they took the batteries out of the school buses?" he barked into the phone. "Gotta go," he told me. "Crazy ass town."

He kissed me and left Tea Time.

"The cop's a good catch," Ruth told me when Spencer was gone. "But he's crap where bubble gum's concerned. You okay? Your face is doing something weird."

"Again?"

"Come with me."

"Where?"

"Follow me. Come on. I won't bite you."

"Put that in writing."

She ignored me, and I followed her into the back of the shop and up the back stairs. "Is this where you live? You're letting me into your home? Are you feeling okay? Should I call a doctor? What am I supposed to do for a stroke? Aspirin? CPR? Oh, God, Ruth, please don't tell me that I have to do mouth-to-mouth on you."

She stopped at a door and shot me a death stare. "Very funny, Gladie. I'm letting you in, but don't touch anything. You touch something, I cut your hands off. You understand?"

I nodded. Ruth had been slightly less aggressive in recent months, but I wouldn't have put it past her to cut my hands off. She was hardcore.

"Whoa. This is nice," I said, walking into her apartment.

"Don't touch anything."

"These are antiques, right?"

"Don't touch them."

"Are they French?"

"American, Gladie. Don't you know anything? Western American. Your heritage. Your people came here during the gold rush, same as mine."

"Really?" I asked her. "Our families have known each other for over one hundred years?"

"Sit over there." Ruth pointed to a small couch, which looked like it had come out of a John Wayne movie.

"I can't sit on it without touching it."

"Shut up and sit down."

"Okay, just warning you that if I sit down, I'll be touching it."

Ruth put her hands on her hips and scrunched up her face. "Sit down, or I'm getting my Louisville Slugger."

I put my hands up in surrender. "Just messing with you, Ruth. I have to have some fun."

I sat down, and Ruth sat next to me. "I heard what Spencer said to you. You know, about your father. I've decided to tell you about that day."

I stopped breathing. I was shocked to my core. I never expected her to talk about my father's accident.

"I've never spoken about it. Never." She adjusted her position on the couch, as if she couldn't get comfortable. I couldn't get comfortable, either. I was hanging on her every word, and I had turned toward her like I was squeezing orange juice out of my ass.

"Your father was a no account, you know that, right?" Ruth continued. "But I loved him like he was my own son." She took a linen handkerchief out of her trouser pocket and wiped her eyes. "I'm not crying. I just have something in my eye."

"Me, too," I said, wiping my eyes with the back of my

hand.

"There was just something about that boy, and I knew him since he was in diapers, you know. Knew him before that, when he was in your Grandma's belly like Bridget's baby is now. He used to give me lip. When he was five, he would walk to my shop by himself, and I would give him Earl Grey with a big chunk of rock sugar. When he was eleven, he stole my entire stock of scones and sold them in town, taking the profits to buy himself a stack of comic books and enough Hershey bars to rot out his teeth. When I finally caught up to him after that, I made him sweep my store every morning for three months. That showed him because he hated hard work more than anything, but he did it, and he would charm the socks off me every day that he did. He was like that, you know. Precocious. Rebellious. He was his own drummer, and he learned everything the hard way. When he decided to become a poet, well, what else would he choose to be? Sometimes he would visit me late at night and read to me what he was working on. He was made of magic, that Jonathan Burger. Pure magic."

"But his magic didn't protect him," I said.

"The day his motorcycle went kablooey, and Jonathan died, the old Chief of Police called me to the scene. He didn't want to upset Zelda, you see. And even back then your mother wasn't the most stable woman on the planet. So, I went to identify your father. The whole way there I made deals with the universe that it wouldn't be him. But it was. His bike was a tangled mess of metal, and he was a tangled mess of a man. Bloody. Bruised. But it was him."

I sucked in air. "Yes. That's what Spencer said."

"You had your doubts? That's why you had him look into it?"

How much should I tell her? I didn't know.

"I'll tell you this," Ruth continued without waiting for me to answer. "I never liked those friends of his, and the old Chief never questioned any of them."

"Which friends?" I asked, sitting up straight.

"They were all attached at the hip. They all wanted to be intellectual writers of one type or another. I see a couple of them from time to time. Roman Strand was one of them."

"*The* Roman Strand? The writer?" I wasn't a big reader, but you had to live under a rock not to have heard of Roman Strand. He had written a blockbuster that had won every literary award on the planet.

"That's the one. Rich as Roosevelt. Something fishy about that one. Never looks me in the eye. The rest of them are fishy, too. The only reason I'm telling you is that you have a gift for fishy, and maybe it's time to stick your nose in."

I thought back to my father's notes about faking his death. Why had he written them? Was that his plan, but he died before he could make it happen? And what did his friends have to do with it? "What do you mean they're fishy?"

"Your father built his own motorcycle. He started riding it when his feet could reach the pedals. The day he was killed, there wasn't a cloud in the sky, the sun was shining overhead, and there wasn't another car on the road.

Something happened that wasn't kosher. Fishy."

The hair on my arms stood on end, and a shiver went up my spine. "What else can you tell me about his friends?"

"Nothing. But there's one person who was there for all of it. You need to start with her."

"With who?"

My stomach was filled with lunch and a large latte, but I was craving chocolate in a big way. Either that or a lobotomy to excise the advice that Ruth had given me. I didn't want to go the route she suggested, but now that I had opened Pandora's box, I had to get down to the nitty-gritty fishiness of my father's life and death.

After I finished speaking with Ruth, I drove home. I bypassed Grandma as quickly as I could to race upstairs to the attic. My grandmother seemed slightly suspicious, but the wedding and all things love were keeping her distracted enough so that she didn't ask any questions.

Once I was in the attic, I looked at my father's journal again.

Motorcycle accident.

Injuries too great to identify the body.

Man runs away to a new life, leaving his family behind.

There it was in black and white. I hadn't read it wrong the first time. But with a clearer head, I could now continue reading. Below, my father had scribbled another note in his cat scratch, which was almost impossible to make out. Three words.

Not gonna happen.

Not gonna happen. Not gonna happen? Why did he write it if it wasn't gonna happen? Was he trying to convince himself not to do it?

But he didn't do it. He didn't fake his death. He did die in the motorcycle accident.

My arms sprouted goosebumps. The notes were his but the words weren't. He was noting what someone said to him. A threat. He had been threatened, and he noted it down. He noted down a threat, and then he died.

Perhaps my father's accident wasn't an accident.

Who had threatened him? I had no clue. I didn't know anything about his life or his friends. Damn it. I was going to have to follow Ruth's advice and ask you-know-who.

There was a loud noise outside, and I looked out the window to see if Spencer's house—I mean our house—was okay. Two teenagers ran down the street, each holding what I would have bet money were school bus batteries. In the distance, I heard a police siren. Marked car, not like Spencer's work car. One of the kids turned onto a yard and ducked behind the house. The other kid kept running down our street. I recognized him. It was the teenager who had tricked me into helping him steal bubble gum.

I should have been angry at him, but something in me connected to his civil disobedience. And stealing gum and school bus batteries was funny.

"Up here!" I shouted. He looked up, and I waved. "I'll meet you at the door!"

I jogged downstairs and met him at the door, pulling him into the house right before the police car raced by. "Thanks," he said, breathlessly. "Do I know you?"

"I'm Gladie. I rode on your shoulders yesterday when you stole bubble gum from the convenience store."

"Oh, yeah. You're lighter than you look."

I sucked in my stomach. "Thank you. What are you doing?"

"I'm in the resistance. DICK wants to turn us into zombies. I'm not a zombie. I'm Draco."

"Draco?"

"My mom's a Harry Potter fan. Can I put this down? It's kind of heavy."

"Put it there," Grandma told him, coming into the entranceway. She pointed at the floor by the door. "Stay clear of the window. They're going to come back around slower this time."

"Are you a witch?" he asked her.

Grandma shrugged. "Tomato, tomahto." He put the battery down. "You hungry? We were just about to have a snack," she told him.

We followed her into the kitchen. A huge spread was laid out on the kitchen table. "A new restaurant opened in town," Grandma explained. "They brought over their entire menu and asked me to leave a review with Michael Phelps."

"The Olympic swimmer?" I asked.

Grandma shrugged. "It sounded funny to me, too."

"Michael Phelps?" Draco asked. "You mean Yelp? You're supposed to leave a review on Yelp?"

My grandmother touched her lips. "Maybe he said Yelp. But that doesn't make any more sense than Michael Phelps."

"Yelp," Draco said looking from my grandmother to me and back again. "Yelp. Yelp. Yelp. You haven't heard of Yelp? C'mon. Yelp." Grandma and I stared back at him, blank-faced. "You know…Yelp," he persisted. "Yelp. How can you not know about Yelp? Yelp. Yelp. Yelp."

"I don't think repeating it is going to make us understand it any better," I said.

"It sounds funny," Grandma said. "Yelp? It can't be that. Michael Phelps sounds a lot more logical."

"Is this a joke?" Draco demanded. "Have I landed in an alternate universe? Yelp. C'mon…Yelp."

"Give it up," I told him. "Best thing is sit back, eat, and ask no questions."

"But it's Yelp."

I shrugged. "I don't want to blow your mind completely, but we have a landline, too."

We sat down and consumed an enormous amount of free food. "I'm going to tell Michael Phelps to go to this restaurant, and I'm putting it on my delivery list," Grandma announced. "No fried chicken, but they make killer chili cheese fries."

"Hey Draco, I know you're busy trying to take down DICK, but if you have any time, can I hire you to help me with my laptop and some data entry?" I asked him.

"You mean, like, real money?"

My grandmother's head popped up. She had chili on her chin, but her eyes were focused entirely on me. "You're going to visit your mother in prison?" she asked me, nonplussed.

CHAPTER 6

Every now and then, you're going to get a real kvetcher match that you're going to want to throw out the window. You know the kind…nothing's ever good enough for them. They would complain about winning the lottery. When you get one of these, you might want to give up on them, but here's a little advice from me to you: Even kvetches deserve love. And sometimes with a little love, even a kvetch can become lovable.

Lesson 137, Matchmaking advice from your Grandma Zelda

Yikes. Somehow, my grandmother had picked up that I was going to visit my mother. I didn't want to, but Ruth told me to go to her first to investigate my father's murder, so I was going to. I didn't think that my grandmother could read minds, but just in case, I tried to think about sand to put her off the scent. *Sand. Sand. Sand.* "I thought it would be nice to visit my mother," I lied to her. *Sand. Sand. Sand.* "You know, because of Mother's Day."

"Mother's Day was last month," Draco said. "Wow, you guys need help."

Grandma cocked her head to the side and looked at me with her laser eyes, probably trying to get into my brain to see what I was thinking. *Sand. Sand. Sand.*

I stood up. *Sand. Sand. Sand.* "I'm stuffed. Grandma, this was awesome. Tell Michael Phelps for me. Draco, come with me, and I'll show you what I want."

Upstairs, Draco paused at the entrance to the attic. "You guys aren't serial killers, are you?" he asked.

"I'm ninety-percent sure that we're not serial killers," I said. "I just need computer help."

"I'm not a computer geek."

"But you're young. Young people know computers."

He shrugged and stepped inside. I held up my laptop. "It won't turn on. It turned on before, but now it won't."

Faced with the possibility of pushing a button, Draco was unable to resist. He sat down at the folding table, took my laptop from me, and pushed a button. "It's on," he said.

I looked at the screen. "How did you do that?"

"Is that all you want me to do?"

"No. I need help going through some boxes and put it into the computer in a list. Have you heard of Excel before?"

"Boring."

"I'll pay you."

"My parents pay me."

Millennials. I couldn't make them out. They lived with their families until they were well into adulthood, sponging off the free rent and food. I would have never done that.

Oh, wait.

"Fair enough," I said. "How about I don't tell DICK where you are, and I give you free food, too."

Draco perked up. "My parents eat paleo."

I put my hand on his shoulder. "Draco, I can assure you that there's no paleo food anywhere in this house."

"Okay. Deal."

We made a deal for him to start the next morning, and I promised to drive him home. As he turned to leave, he knocked my father's box onto the floor. "I'll get that," I said, upset to see my father's souvenirs strewn over the dirty attic floor.

"I'll help," Draco said, dropping to his knees. "This is matchmaking stuff?"

"Not this box," I murmured. I felt a pang of protectiveness, like a pit bull protecting a dump.

"*Don't do this, Jonathan,*" Draco read, reading from a scrap of paper. "*Nothing good will come from it. And if you persist, you will have to be stopped.*" Draco waved it at me. "Wow, hardcore. Matchmaking's gangster. Who's Jonathan? You ever get one of these things? Bamboo shoots under your fingernails from angry desperate singles? Bomb threats? The Isis of love. Is matchmaking that sort of thing?"

I took the paper from him. It had been typed on an

old, manual typewriter. Another three sentences. I was learning about my father three sentences at a time. I read it over five times, trying to make sense out of it.

Nope. I couldn't figure it out.

In a moment of whatever the opposite of lucidity is, I asked the juvenile delinquent wearing a *No One Cares* t-shirt what it meant. "Isis of Love? You think it's a threat?"

"Dude." That said it all, and really, I didn't need his opinion. It was definitely a threat.

"I'll take you home," I said, putting the scrap of paper in my purse.

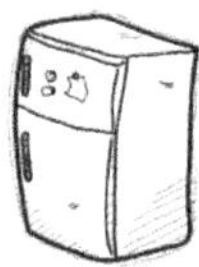

Draco rode in the passenger seat with the school bus battery on his lap. "We have to put the battery back," I told him, driving toward the school bus lot outside of town. "I don't want you to wind up in juvy. I feel responsible for you since I'm feeding you."

"No way. Stealing the bus batteries is genius. DICK wants us to behave. Now, we can't even get to school."

"You can walk to school from anywhere in Cannes," I pointed out.

"It's the thought that counts." Draco sucked in air. "Get down! There they are!"

Draco slumped in his seat. "Who? Who?" I asked looking around.

"DICK!"

"Where? Where?"

"The ones wearing the sweaters with the buttons."

"You mean cardigans?" Sure enough there was a group of three middle-aged women and one elderly man walking on the sidewalk, and they were all wearing cardigans. "So, that's DICK, huh?"

"They're everywhere," Draco said. "But we're going to show them."

"They don't look very scary, Draco. They'll probably get tired and go home, wherever that is."

"I heard they're from Utah or a state next to it, like New Hampshire."

We arrived at the bus lot, and I stopped the car next to a school bus, which had its hood up. "All righty. Put the battery back in the bus," I told him.

"I can't."

"C'mon. We're not leaving until you do it."

"No, I mean, I can't. I don't know how."

"Don't you take auto shop in school?"

"What's auto shop?"

"I can't believe this," I said, opening my door. "Fine. I'll do it. At least bring out the battery for me."

We got out, and I climbed onto the bus's front bumper. Looking inside, I realized I had no idea how to install a battery, either. But at least there was an obvious gaping hole where the battery went. "I'll just put it in here, and they can fix the wires, later," I told Draco. "Hand me the battery."

He handed it to me, and I worked to let it down into the motor. It was a good plan, but it was harder than I had expected. I had to practically crawl inside to get access. I see-sawed over the lip of the hood, trying to put the battery in without damaging the motor.

"You should probably go faster," Draco said. "Yep, going faster would be really good right about now."

"I'm going as fast as I'm going to go. Instead of complaining, why don't you come up here and help me? I could use some help. Come on, Draco. Draco? Draco? Draco, are you there?"

There was no answer. I struggled to turn around, but I lost my balance and fell face-first into the bowels of the bus. "Draco, help me out of here," I said, but there was still no sign of him.

"Hurry, Officer!" I heard a woman yell. "They're at it, again! Stop! Decency in Cannes Kids! Decency in Cannes Kids!"

Someone tugged at my foot and came away with my shoe. "Get out of there!" another woman yelled. "Decency…"

"In Cannes Kids!" I finished for her. "Yeah. Yeah. I get it, but I can't get out of here."

"Officer, it's happening, again. This town is rotten to the core." This time it was a man talking. How many people were out there? "This boy's butt is out for everyone to see," the man announced.

"My butt doesn't look anything like a boy's butt," I

complained.

"She's right," I heard a voice that I recognized say. "I know that butt. It's no boy's butt."

"Whose butt is it?" I heard another woman ask. "Do you know that butt?"

"Don't you recognize that butt, Margie?" he asked her.

There was a short pause. "I do sort of recognize it," she said. "Hold on. Is that the Chief's butt?"

"Yep. The Chief's butt."

"I'm not the Chief's butt!" I insisted. "Help me out of here. I have a mouth full of radiator."

The smell of cologne and a boatload of testosterone wafted toward me, and Remington's head joined mine under the hood. "That's not the radiator, babe."

"Throw the book at her," a woman yelled. "It's time for justice in this town and for law-abiding citizens to breathe free."

"I don't have a book to throw at you," Remington whispered to me and winked. "Looking good, Gladie. High and tight, as usual. Don't tell the Chief I told you that."

"Stealing school bus batteries is a federal crime!" one of the DICK ladies announced.

"On second thought, maybe you shouldn't help me out of here," I whispered to Remington.

"Captain Kirk would never let a damsel in distress stay stuck under the hood of a school bus," he said and lifted me out of the bus like I was light as air and put me down gently on the blacktop next to the bus.

There was a sea of cardigans, and they were all pointing at me. "It's not what it looks like," I said, but I didn't even sound convincing to myself. "I was just trying to help."

"I guess there's no short circuit video this time," Margie said, looking around and shielding her eyes from the sun.

"I was putting the battery back," I insisted.

"You stole it and had second thoughts?" she asked.

I shot Remington a look, and he shrugged. "I just work here," he told me.

"I was just trying to help. Look," I said, turning toward Remington. "How about you let me go, and you don't tell Spencer about this?"

Remington looked down at me through his steely, dark eyes and shrugged, again. "There's a lot I'd like to not tell him."

"Tell me about what? What do you not want him to tell me?"

The voice boomed past the DICK voices, which were demanding my lynching or whatever torture and punishment they envisioned for my crimes. Only one voice could outvoice so many cardigans. It was the man I loved. The man I was going to marry. The man who was building a house for me. The man who hated when I wreaked havoc on the town.

I turned toward his voice, and there he was perfectly dressed in his Armani suit, his hair perfectly cut and perfectly slightly disheveled. His body tall and muscular, not as much as Remington, but impressive nonetheless and perfectly proportioned. His face was sharp and angular, his expression quick to move between fun and flirty and imposing and ferocious.

He was leaning toward the imposing and ferocious right now.

"Are you kidding me?"

"It's not what it looks like," I told him.

"She's the ringleader," one of the DICK women shrieked. "She was caught red-handed, stealing school bus batteries. She's probably the ringleader of the bubble gum bandits, too."

Another DICK woman waved a lock of her hair in Spencer's face. "I got bubble gum in my hair from those heathens. The only way to get it out is to cut it out. Do you know how long it'll take me to grow back this much hair at my age? Forever, that's how long! Decency! We need decency here!"

"I have bubble gum stuck to my private hair," a DICK man announced. "A person shouldn't have anything stuck to their private hair. It's private! We must bring decency back to this town."

"Let's start with *her*!"

"Lock her up!"

"This is getting ugly," Margie said. "I thought Cannes was relaxing. I moved here for the Cannes Needlepoint Society. I wanted to needlepoint until I die in a nice relaxing setting."

"I didn't know you did needlepoint," Remington said to her. "Can you make me a Princess Leia in her metal bikini needlepoint pillow?"

"Sure. That shouldn't be too hard."

"Arrest her!" a DICK man yelled.

"Use shackles, not those wimpy handcuffs!" another DICK man yelled.

"They use zip-ties now, Ralph."

"Like they use for bread? This country is going to hell in a handbasket."

At that moment, I was so happy that I was sleeping with the Chief of police. It was only a matter of minutes before DICK was going to bring out the tar and feathers, and I needed all of the allies I could get.

Throughout the shouts to hang me from the rafters, Spencer never took his eyes off me. His ferocious look of *Lucy, you have some splainin' to do* had changed to his normal little smirk that seemed to say: "I know how you look naked with your feet behind your ears."

"I was putting the battery back," I told him. "I was trying to help."

"You were being a good Samaritan," he agreed.

"Exactly."

"You decided to do some auto work, even though you've never changed a tire or even checked your oil."

"I worked in a car wash for one afternoon in Memphis."

Spencer nodded. "If I let you go, there'll be a riot. I have to make a show of it."

"But I'm on my way to visit my mother."

Spencer gasped and took a step backward. "Why?" he asked, freaked out. "Are you sick? Oh my God, are you like Bridget?"

I sucked in my stomach. "No, I'm not like Bridget," I screeched. "I don't have to wait until I'm preg...preg... you know what, to visit my mother."

Spencer shrugged. "Fine, I'll take you and Remington will take your car home. I'll make a show like I'm arresting you."

"But..."

"Or I could feed you to the cardigans."

The DICK mob had surrounded us, and I would have bet money that if they had access to some firewood and a lighter, I was going to go up in flames like it was Salem in the 1600s. "Fine. Take me to see my mother."

I handed the keys to Remington, and Spencer made a big show of handcuffing me and putting me in the back of his car, after he got my shoe back. It wasn't the first time that I was humiliated in front of a large crowd, and it probably wouldn't be the last, so while he was announcing to the DICK people to disperse because law enforcement had everything in hand, I thought about my father.

What had he gotten into? He was a poet, and as far as I knew, poets didn't attract a lot of enemies except for those who didn't like poetry. But even the people who didn't like poetry didn't actively go after poets. At least I didn't think so. I had only known one poet in my life.

Spencer was quiet as we drove out of town. Once we were past DICK territory, he pulled the car over, dragged me out, and uncuffed me. "I'm thinking I have a brain tumor from my cellphone or something because seeing you almost stoned to death by a bunch of out-of-towner old biddies got me real hot. How about you? You hot?"

"I have school bus grease in my hair, and one of the DICK people spat in my eye."

Spencer pushed me up against the car and rubbed his magical enlarging pelvis on me. "So, what does that mean? You're hot, too?"

"I could be hot," I started. "Wait a minute. No. No, I'm not hot. Whatever happened to wining and dining me? What happened to romance?"

"We could stop for burgers after I have my way with you."

I put my hands on his chest, making an inch of space between us. "Again, not very romantic. Besides, visiting hours at the prison end soon. I don't have a lot of time."

"Perfect. I can be in and out in about twenty seconds. Plenty of time to get to the prison before it closes."

"You make it sound like you're going to take a quick shower."

"Yes, but a lot dirtier. Come on, Pinky. Give a guy a break. These DICK people are driving me crazy. And there's bubble gum on every surface in town. Look at my Prada shoes. They'll never be the same."

"I can't believe I'm marrying a guy who wears Prada shoes. I got my shoes from the Walley's Super Sale Dumpster on the sidewalk outside of the store. They cost $2.50. I had to fight a homeless man for them, and I paid for the shoes with dimes and nickels."

"I love when you talk dirty to me, Pinky."

"I still have a bruise on my arm from that fight with the homeless guy," I said, showing him the bruise.

"You want me to kiss it and make it better?"

"Okay," I said, my body swimming in a sea of Spencer hormones.

"How about if I start kissing a lot lower and make my way to your arm?"

It sounded good, but there was something I was forgetting about. Oh, yeah. I woke up from his seductive charm. If I gave in for his request for a quickie, I couldn't get done what I needed to do. I pushed hard against him, making him take two steps back. "Visiting hours!"

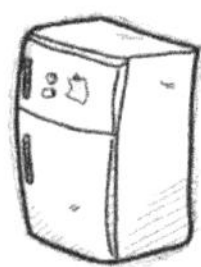

The state had moved my mother to a progressive prison farm up in the mountains, not far from Cannes. There, inmates ran an organic farm because caring for goats and cows was supposed to be great for rehabilitation. I didn't know if it was working in my mother's case because I hadn't spoken to her since she was arrested for operating a mobile meth lab on a used moped.

"I want to see her by myself," I told Spencer when we walked inside, and he flashed his badge in order to get us special service.

"Okay, but stay away from her mouth."

"Is that code?" I asked him.

"She's bitten a few people since she's been incarcerated. Although, it's been all quiet on the western front since she's been at this farm."

"How do you know that?"

"I've been keeping tabs on her."

"You have?"

"Su casa es mi casa," he said, as if that said it all, and I supposed it did. He had staked his claim to everything that was my life, and he was determined to take care of me and make sure my life ran smoothly.

Poor bastard.

A guard escorted me through the grounds of the farm. The prison was a square of one-story buildings with the farm in the center. Inmates wore blue jeans and yellow and green striped shirts. It was nerve-racking having prisoners walking free near me, but I figured the farm was just for stupid criminals like my mother who made meth on mopeds.

I didn't hold out a lot of hope that my mother could shed light on my father's death. After all, after he died, she turned inward and to the bottle. She wouldn't feel the need to do me any favors, and I wasn't even sure that she cared about my father or why he died any longer, if she ever did.

"Here she is," the guard told me.

"Where?" I asked, looking around.

"There." The guard pointed at a young woman, pulling weeds in a vegetable garden. She looked nothing like my mother. She was younger, more relaxed. Sober. Then, she touched her chin in a way that made me flashback to my childhood. An image of my mother working with my grandmother's rosebushes flashed through my brain. She leaned over the roses, laughed and cut a pretty pink flower, handing it to me and warning me to be careful of the thorns. And she touched her chin in just this way.

"Mom?" I asked.

The woman in the vegetable garden turned and smiled at me. "Gladie, I'm so happy to see you," she said, standing. She wiped her hands on her jeans.

"Mom, are they drugging you?"

"Drugging me with clean air and good, honest work," she said, still smiling.

Then, my mother did something she hadn't done in years. She hugged me.

CHAPTER 7

Third eye or no third eye, people will shock the shit out of you, dolly.

Lesson 68, Matchmaking advice from your Grandma Zelda

We sat cross-legged between rows of chamomile tea plants. My mother told me I looked good, and that she was happy and was learning Tai Chi. I tried to shut my mouth, but my jaw kept dropping open. Finally, after her telling me how wonderful her life was in prison, I got around to asking her if she ever thought my father's accident was suspicious.

"I never stopped thinking it was suspicious," she said, and a tear rolled down her cheek, which she wiped away, self-consciously. The powers and longevity of grief are amazing. Even Superman couldn't take on this supervillain.

"Did Dad have any enemies? Maybe someone out to

get him?"

"Everyone loved your father. He was so full of life. He was bursting with it. And folks wanted to grab some of that life that was bursting out of him." She touched her chin and looked up at the sky and then back at me. "Have you noticed that most folks are only about three-fourths full of life? The rest is death, creeping up on them like mold. So, they search out life, like a man searching for water in the desert. Well, there was your father, overflowing with life, and wherever he went, people attached themselves to him. He was like a magnet. When he left, all that life was snuffed out. I had never thought such a thing was possible, Gladie. But there you go. Impossible happens morning, noon, and night in this world."

She took a jagged breath and wiped at her eyes again. I was tempted to reach out and touch her, to console her. But we didn't have that relationship, and I couldn't bring myself to touch her.

"So, he didn't have any enemies, nobody who wanted to hurt him?"

"Jonathan was tied to the hips of five fast friends. They would sit around your grandmother's parlor every night until three in the morning and talk about Blake and Sartre and who knew what else. I never even graduated high school, so I just sat there like a lump on a log not understanding a word until I fell asleep."

"Five friends? Why didn't I ever meet them?"

"Oh, you did. You knew all of them until your father

died. Then, they disappeared."

Her face changed from sadness to anger. "What do you mean, they disappeared?" I asked.

"Exactly. It's crazy that five friends that I had seen most every day since I met your father suddenly disappeared. You know what I think? I think it was a guilty conscious. I think that one of them killed Jonathan. They couldn't stand that he had more life in him than all of them put together and they decided to snuff it out. One of those friends took your father's life."

I had stopped breathing, as I listened to my mother. "How? I thought he had a motorcycle accident."

"He died on his motorcycle, but as far as I know, they never proved it was an accident. And there's another thing, Gladie. That motorcycle just up and disappeared afterward. No one ever saw it, again."

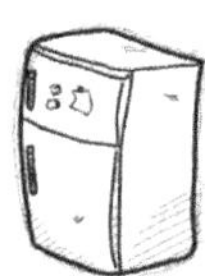

It was the longest conversation that I had ever had with my mother. By the time I left her at the prison farm, I had the complete certainty that my father was murdered, and I had a list of his friends, who were the most obvious suspects. I debated with myself whether to tell Spencer the reason I had visited my mother, but when he saw me, he put his arms around me and drove me home without saying a word, which made the decision for me.

On the way home, we stopped for hamburgers, just like he had promised, and then we went home where I tried to wash the day off of me and slept in Spencer's arms.

The next morning, I skipped breakfast to avoid my grandmother, because I was sure she could at least read on my face what I was up to. After Spencer left for work, I called Lucy.

"Are you up for some sleuthing?"

"Who died?"

"My father."

"Oh, right. Yes! Harry's got the boys over for poker, so this is perfect." Harry's "boys" were all at least seventy-years-old, and they all looked like they had jumped out of a *Godfather* movie. "You want me to pick you up, or are you going to pick me up?"

"I'll come get you. Do you have any coffee and maybe an egg sandwich?"

I tracked down the first name on my mother's list. Adam Mancuso. He was some kind of writer, but my mother didn't think he was a poet. In any case, I didn't have to Google him or look him up on Facebook, because he had never left Cannes, and I found his address easily in the phone book. He lived outside the Historic District by the lake.

I picked up Lucy in her fancy neighborhood, and she greeted me with a cup of coffee and an egg sandwich. "Where are we going?" she asked, getting into my car. "I've got a Taser in my purse, just in case we run into trouble."

I gave her the rundown on my father's friends and showed her the list. "I know two of these people," Lucy said. "Roman Strand and Joy Lennon. But now she's Joy Strand. They're married and live in a humdinger of a mansion down the street from me. He's a big deal. I saw him on *Good Morning America*."

Damn it. We had driven right past it, and we were almost to the lake, too far to turn around. "What are they like?" I asked Lucy.

"Harry invited Roman to his poker game when we first moved into the neighborhood, but Roman said he was too busy. Actually, Joy said he was too busy. She sent a note to our house. I gather she organizes the house while he's busy being a literary genius. And she likes Botox. I've seen her getting in and out of her car, but that's it."

I felt a pang of jealousy, hearing about the success of my father's friend. It wasn't fair that Roman got to live a long life, be thought of as a literary genius, and appear on *Good Morning America* while my father was cut down in the prime of his life.

I stopped the car by a dirt side road. "Is this it?" I asked.

"Looks like the perfect road for a killer to live on. Secluded back road. I have a good feeling about this, darlin'."

Lucy was practically drooling over the idea of tracking down a killer. She was wearing a poufy peach organza dress and peach, leather pumps. Her hair was perfectly done, and I imagined she must have spent a thousand dollars a month in upkeep maintenance. Normally I would have had the same enthusiasm for solving a mystery and bringing a killer to justice, but this was different. This was personal and every step I made closer to discovering the truth about my father's last moments brought new pain. But, pain aside, I felt the familiar drive to get down to the truth and find the dirty, lowdown murderer who took my father from me.

"Are you okay, Gladie?" Lucy asked, "Your face turned red."

"Fine. I was just thinking."

"You have that look, again. The Miss Marple look. Oh, this is going to be so good."

There was a mailbox at the entrance to the road, which meant that someone must have lived at the end of it. I turned onto the dirt road.

"I'm revving up my Taser," Lucy announced. "If you distract him, I'll fill him full of volts."

The house came into view, as we continued to drive down the road. "Hold on there, Annie Oakley, as far as we know, Adam Mancuso is just an old friend of my father's."

"So, should I turn off the Taser?"

"No. Keep it charged. If he tries anything, I'll kick

him in the balls, and you light him up."

Adam's house was a sprawling cabin that looked like it had been built piecemeal, added onto when the mood struck. It was made with different kinds of wood, and the cabin stood at different heights. Smoke came out of two chimneys on either side of the house. The road had turned from dirt to gravel as we reached the makeshift driveway. I turned off the car, and Lucy and I stepped out.

"Don't make any sudden movements, darlin'," Lucy said, putting her arms around me. I looked in the direction she was staring, alarmed. Coming toward us was a large, pointy rodent.

"What is that?" I asked, as we shuffled around the creature on our way to the front door.

"The largest porcupine I've ever seen."

"You've seen porcupines before?"

"I've seen everything."

There wasn't a doorbell, so I knocked on the door. The porcupine walked toward us, but now he had his pointy things standing up tall, ready to shoot us full of holes. It wasn't the way I wanted to die. Actually, I didn't want to die at all, but if I was going to die, I wanted to die by something much faster than being stabbed to death with animal parts.

The door opened, and a man wearing dirty sweatpants and a Walley's t-shirt stood staring at me, as if he was confused that there were other humans on the planet, and even more confused that those humans would knock on his door. His feet were bare, and his shoulder-length hair was doing a bed-head thing.

"I don't want to be a Jehovah's Witness," he said, like he was apologizing.

"We're not here to convert you," Lucy said. "This is Gladie Burger. Jonathan's daughter."

He blinked and then blinked again. "Jonathan?" he asked, looking at me.

"Do you mind if we come in? There's a porcupine after us." Lucy pushed past him, and we walked into the house.

It was dark inside, but even without a lot of light, it was obvious that Adam wasn't overly concerned with tidiness. Or cleanliness.

Adam was a slob.

But Adam was rich. Everything in his house was luxury, custom made. The entrance gave way to a great room with the kitchen part to my left. The fancy, filthy kitchen seemed to call to me, and I found myself inspecting the appliances on the counter top. "Is this the Rockefeller Remote Control Six-Setting Popcorn Maker?" I asked Adam.

"Seven-settings. It's the newest version."

"I could go for some popcorn," I said. "Oh my God, tell me I'm not seeing the JP Morgan Automatic Panini Maker with Built in Cheese Dispenser." It was like I was Dorothy, and I had fallen into an Oz filled with wonderful appliances.

"It makes a ham and cheese panini in fifteen seconds," he said. "Panini means grilled cheese. Is that why you're here?"

"Yes," I said, but Lucy shot me a mean Confederate look, like she was mad about my northern aggression and was going to impale me with her bayonet. "I mean, no. I came to talk to you about my father."

Adam ran his hand over his hair and blinked a lot. "Oh, wow. I haven't talked about Jonathan in years. He's dead. I mean, yeah, you know that."

Adam wasn't coming off as the grand, arch villain genius who planned my father's murder. But I had known other clueless, idiot killers, so I refused to be taken in.

"I'm going through his old friends, talking to everyone," I said.

"Good idea. We were very close. You want a cream soda?" he asked.

"Sure. Thanks."

He took a couple out of his refrigerator. I drank from the can because his glasses were dirty. "It's French," Adam said, pointing at the cream soda can.

"Really? It's still good, though."

Adam nodded. "Your dad was the best friend a guy could have. I would never be who I am without him." He took a large butcher paper-wrapped package out of the refrigerator. A gigantic aquarium with one kind of fish swimming in it filled an entire wall. Adam climbed a ladder and dumped the package's contents into the water. It made a bloody cloud, and the fish swarmed around it. It was gone within seconds.

Lucy mouthed "Taser" to me and tapped her purse.

"Piranhas," Adam explained. "Ultra cool, but it costs a fortune to feed them. So, what do you want to know?"

"The police are looking into my father's death," I lied, more than a little disconcerted by the piranhas. "Or should I say…murder." I waited for a response, but he was still doing the *duh* thing coupled with a vacant stare. "Because it's suspicious, you know."

"It is? It was?" Adam backed up until he was leaning against the kitchen counter. He tapped a finger against his mouth, as if he was thinking. "You know, the accident *was* weird. Tragic and weird. I think you're right. Afterward, it was like Jonathan never existed, and our group all spread to the four winds. I've never spoken to any of them, again, even though we were all best friends at the time." He looked up at the ceiling. "That's not true. Steve contacted me a couple times over the years to buy insurance. That's what he does now. He works at Cannes Fidelity above the pharmacy."

"I know that place. I know that guy," I said, pointing at Adam. We had bumped into each other in the pharmacy's Pop-Tart aisle, and he tried to sell me life insurance because Pop-Tart eaters lived seven years less than non Pop-Tart eaters, according to him. Of course, I figured he was insane, grabbed my S'mores Pop-Tarts, and left.

"Did you threaten Jonathan?" Lucy demanded, wagging her finger at him, in a burst of savage aggression, like she was Jessica Fletcher. "Did you sabotage his motorcycle, leaving his wife a widow, and his daughter an orphan? Spit it out. Tell us the truth."

"No! I loved him. He was my best friend. He helped me build a bathroom onto this house. And he supported my writing when nobody else said I could succeed. We talked about writing every day."

"What about the rest of your circle of friends?" I asked, more gently than Lucy. "Would any of them threaten my father?"

"Everyone loved him."

Adam wiped his face with a kitchen towel and took a swig of his cream soda. The conversation was over, and I was no closer to finding the truth out about my father's death. All I found out was my father knew how to build a bathroom.

"Anything else? I have to get back to work," Adam said. There was a loud noise from somewhere in the house, and Lucy stepped toward it. Adam put his arm out to block her. "I can't let you back there. Too dangerous. Komodo dragon."

"I get it, now," Lucy told him. "You collect dangerous pets."

"Danger is in the eye of the beholder," he said. "Just because someone is a man-eater or viciously aggressive doesn't mean they don't deserve to be loved."

"I kind of think it does," Lucy said.

CHAPTER 8

I like to think of matchmaking as the most glamorous job in the world, second only to shoe designer. But the whole megillah isn't a crash whiz bang of excitement one hundred percent of the time. Sometimes, matchmaking is a slow slog full of researching, like a nudnik who can't get enough. But an ounce of research is worth a pound of do-overs. So, one foot in front of the other. Step by step. Gather your information and then you'll be the success I'll know you'll be, bubbeleh.

Lesson 129, Matchmaking advice from your
Grandma Zelda

I drove back to the Historic District to see Steve Byrne, the second name on my list. Lucy called Bridget to see if she wanted to go with us, but she was busy eating French soft cheeses and watching horror movies to try and make her baby come into the world.

"She's not exactly the poster child for pregnancy," Lucy said, hanging up. "We should go over there later to give her moral support. Or we could send a muffin basket."

"I'm voting for the muffin basket." I needed a half-day break from Bridget's pregnancy. I parked in front of the pharmacy. The front door was covered in DICK posters, which were splattered with chewed globs of bubble gum. "This town is savage," I said.

Lucy put her arm around me, as we walked through the door next to the pharmacy. "This is brave of you. I would never search out my parents' friends. Of course, they're up in the mountains messin' with sheep, so..."

We climbed up the stairs. On the second floor, there was one old-fashioned door with glass in the center. "Cannes Fidelity, Steve Byrne Broker" was written on it in thick, black letters. I knocked on the door and turned the doorknob.

Inside, there was a woman sitting at a desk and reading a magazine. "Lucy Smythe here to see Mr. Byrne," I told her, using Lucy's name in case he would get scared off by my father's last name.

"He's eating lunch."

"I was looking for a complete insurance package," I lied. I had no idea what that meant, but I figured it would be music to Steve's ears. It was. She buzzed him, and he came out, beaming at us.

"Steve Byrne. Happy to make your life more secure." He put his hand out, and I shook it. "Come in. Come in. Take a seat."

We sat, and Steve dropped to his knees and then onto all fours. "Who's a good poopykins? Daddy's baby is a good poopykins. Aren't you? Aren't you? Aren't you a good poopykins?"

I had never bought insurance in an office before, so I didn't know if this was standard business practice or not.

"Daddy loves his baby. Yes, he does," he continued.

A little rat-like dog crawled out from under the desk. It was wearing a diamond collar and an outfit that looking disturbingly like my grandmother's Gucci knockoff dress.

"There she is. There's Daddy's girl. And don't you look pretty today? Would you like to meet our guests? They're going to buy the full insurance package? Yes, that's right. Yes, that's right. That's right, my poopykins."

"I take back what I said," Lucy muttered in my direction. "I'd much prefer to visit my parents' friends in the mountains with the sheep."

Steve put a small, jewel-encrusted throne on his desk and picked up his poopykins and sat her on the throne. "Is Daddy's girl comfortable?" he asked her. He put a bite of his lunch in his mouth and then fed the dog from his mouth. I looked away so I wouldn't throw up.

"Say hello to Lady Philomena, an award-winning bitch."

Lucy elbowed me in the side. "He's talking to us, Gladie. Hello, Lady Philomena."

"Hello, Lady Philomena," I said. "Uh, listen, I might have been a little untruthful about the package. I'm Gladie

Burger, Jonathan Burger's daughter."

He sat on his desk with a loud thump. "Jonathan Burger's daughter. Well, look at that. I was wondering when you would come visit me. After your father died, we all went our separate ways, but I figured you'd at least be curious. I was your father's best friend, you know." He looked beyond me and gnawed at his lower lip. "Okay, maybe not his best friend. I wasn't literary enough for him or the rest of them. I was in the group, but obviously I didn't turn out like they did."

I sat up straighter in my chair. Jealousy. Besides sex and money, it was the best motive for murder. Lucy caught my eye. She had noticed it, too.

"You dad was the king of us," Steve continued. "Three published books of poetry. Do you know how hard that is to do in this country? If he had lived, he would have gone all the way. Nobel Prize. Tenure at Stanford. The whole enchilada. So, he didn't have a lot of time for me. Not like he did for the others."

"I'm sorry," I said. "That must have upset you."

"Really upset you. You probably wanted him dead," Lucy said. Smooth.

"I didn't want him dead, but would a pimple on his face have been too much to ask? He was Paul Newman meets Ted Hughes meets Rock Hudson before he was gay. How does a guy compete with that?"

He leaned over and kissed his dog on the lips. His pants were covered in a light layer of dog hair, and he had a unibrow that moved when he spoke. I felt sorry for him. I understood what it was like to be an underachiever in an overachieving group. It never made me kill anyone, but I also never French kissed a dog. So, Steve Byrne had moved ahead of Adam Mancuso as my number one suspect.

"What do you want to know about him?" he asked me.

"What do you mean?"

"Well, you're here to get information about your dad, right? Closure? That sort of thing."

"The motorcycle," I started.

"He loved that thing. Your mom drove a beat-up Honda Civic, and he roared through town on his cool-mobile. He drove like a bat out of hell. Joy used to joke that he was going to die on it and then his poetry would be worth a fortune. And then he did die. We were all shocked, so shocked that we didn't talk about it. I don't know if you remember, but your father was full of life, and maybe that was why it was so shocking that he died."

"His poetry wasn't worth a fortune after he died," I said.

"Yeah, well, at least he published before he died. Three of us never published and three did. Adam, Roman, and your dad all published. The rest of us weren't so lucky."

He oozed guilt. Or maybe I just didn't like him. But for the time being, I couldn't prove anything. "I'm sorry you weren't published," I said.

Steve shrugged and picked up his dog. "Insurance has

been good to me. Speaking of insurance, how about we get you taken care of while you're here? When I get through with you, I can throw you down the stairs, and you wouldn't have to worry a thing about money for the rest of your life. Your father didn't have a nickel of insurance. You don't want to suffer the same fate, do you?"

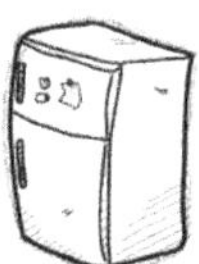

I didn't buy any insurance, and I refused to say goodbye to Lady Philomena. Blech. I wanted to wash myself in Clorox to get the weird off of me.

"I preferred the pet piranhas to the dog," Lucy told me, as we walked across the street to Tea Time. "I've always liked dogs, but that thing in there wasn't a dog."

"The man sure was. A lowdown, dirty dog."

After coffee at Tea Time, I drove Lucy home because Harry was asking for her. When I dropped her off, my cellphone rang, and I answered.

"Is this Gladys Burger?" a woman asked me.

"Gladie Burger. Yes."

"Jonathan Burger's daughter?"

My heart rate sped up, and my mouth got dry. "Yes. Who's this?"

"Joy Strand. I used to be Joy Lennon. I heard that you're making the rounds of our old gang of friends. Roman and I would love to talk with you. I haven't seen you since you were a little girl. There's no chance that you could be free for lunch?"

"I'm free, and I'm actually in your neighborhood."

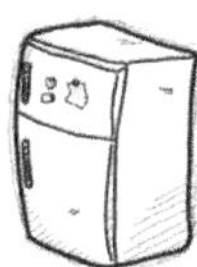

Lucy lived in a mansion, but Roman and Joy Strand lived in an estate that I had always pictured when I thought of a literary titan. Not that I ever thought of a literary titan, but I did know who JK Rowling was. Ditto Stephen King. Lucy let me clean myself up in her house before I went to lunch, and while Harry dealt cards to his old cronies, she gave me an earful about Roman.

"He wrote one book, and that was enough," Lucy said. "I never read it, but I think I own a couple copies. That book's been around for decades, and it must have sold millions and millions of copies. It's like *Fifty Shades* but for people who want to seem intelligent. You know what I mean?"

I nodded. I hadn't read it, either, but I had heard of Roman Strand before, just like everyone else in the world had.

"I'm telling you, Gladie, an invitation into their house is a big deal. I can't get in, and believe you me, I've tried."

At Roman and Joy's house, I rang the doorbell, and there was a loud *ding dong* noise. I was half-expecting a butler to answer, but a heavily Botoxed woman did, instead, who I assumed was Joy. I was right.

She gave me a big, welcoming hug, and I got choked up from the attention from one of my father's friends. "Let me look at you," she said, holding me at arm's length. "Just like your father, except for your coloring. I should have contacted you before, but it was a strange time. Oh! I haven't let you come in, have I?"

She waved me inside with a giggle and closed the door. The walls were paneled in a dark wood, and there was artwork everywhere. Happily, there wasn't an animal anywhere, and I hoped that I had finally found some normal people in my father's group. We walked into the dining room, and a tall man, smoking a pipe, was waiting for us.

"Gladys," he said and opened his arms for me. I walked toward him, and he hugged me. "I've never been happier than I am to see Jonathan's daughter in my home."

He smelled like expensive cologne and something else I couldn't pinpoint. Pot roast. That was it. He smelled like pot roast.

"I hope you like pot roast," Joy said. "That's what we're having for lunch."

I loved pot roast.

We sat down and started to eat. It was delicious. "We heard that you met with Adam and Steve," Joy said. "I hope you weren't too put off by their eccentricities."

"We haven't spoken with them in years, Joy," Roman said. "They might be totally different now."

"Are they?" Joy asked me. "Are they still eccentric?"

I swallowed a piece of pot roast. "A little bit."

Joy laughed. "She's diplomatic, Roman. Did you notice? Not at all like her father. Gladys, your dad didn't have a diplomatic bone in his body."

Roman nodded. "That's what I liked about him. I always knew where he stood, even if I didn't want to. He told me in no uncertain terms."

"We loved your father," Joy told me. "He was so full of life. And so talented."

"Yes, so talented," Roman agreed.

"Did everyone like him?" I asked.

"What do you mean?" Roman asked.

"I mean, is it possible that…I mean, is there a chance that… well, maybe that my father's accident wasn't an accident?"

Nobody blinked. Nobody breathed. Forks hung in the air, halfway to mouths. "Why?" Joy asked, finally. "I thought it was ruled an accident. Have you heard something different?"

"Do the police suspect foul play?" Roman asked, concerned. "I find that hard to believe. Your father was so full of life. Everyone loved him."

"Everyone loved him," Joy agreed.

"Even Steve? I got the impression he was jealous of my father."

Roman laughed. "Steve? He didn't want any of the trappings of family and responsibility that Jonathan had."

"No, Roman. I think Gladys is right," Joy

interrupted. "Steve never managed to finish a book. He had nothing to show for himself, literary-wise. It would be normal for him to be jealous, and maybe just maybe he did something about it."

Roman speared a chunk of pot roast with his fork and put it into his mouth. "I don't think jealousy is a reason to murder."

"Of course not, honey," Joy said. "You have me curious, Gladys. I think it's time to get the whole gang together. Roman and I can help you talk to the others and find out more about your father's accident. Call me crazy, but I think it'll work. Let us help you. How about an informal dinner party tomorrow evening? Would you like that, Gladys?"

All the suspects together in one place? Damn right, I would like that.

"Is that a good idea, Joy?" Roman asked. "It's been years since we've been together."

"Exactly. It's time to catch up and talk about Jonathan's passing once and for all," she said. "And Gladys, feel free to bring your significant other. A little bird told me that you're engaged."

It had been a successful day. I had managed to talk to four of my father's five friends from the list my mother gave me. For whatever reason, they had all welcomed me with one level of enthusiasm or another. I guessed it was a testament to my father that they would take time out of their day to talk to his daughter who was uninvited and unexpected in their lives.

Or they felt guilty. It was one or the other, and I was determined to find out which.

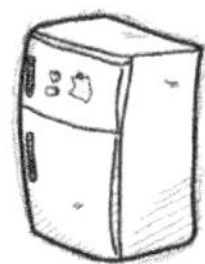

On my way home, I stopped off at Bridget's. She was doing jumping jacks when she opened the door. "Still no labor?" I asked.

"Just the farting kind." She huffed and puffed. I took her by the arm.

"How about you take a break and sit with me on the couch?"

"Okay. I'm tired, anyway."

I brought her a glass a water and got one for me, too. I told her all about my father's friends. "Well?" she asked. "What's your gut telling you? Which one did it?"

"I'm not even sure there was an 'it' that was done."

"Men," she said, as if that said it all.

"So far I have one motive and that's jealousy. That would mean Steve did it."

"Or the weird porcupine, dragon guy," Bridget suggested. "But in this political climate, the uber rich couple probably did it."

Bridget rearranged her body on the couch, putting her swollen feet on my lap. I started to massage them. "Have you decided on a name for the baby, yet?" I asked. She had gone through the name of every labor rights activist since the beginning of time.

"Not, yet. A name is important, Gladie. What if Martin Luther King had been named Adolph? Totally different outcome."

"You have a point."

"I wish my feet weren't so swollen. Then, I could help the young people take on those fascist, authoritarian, jack-booted nasty people who invaded the town."

"DICK."

She pushed her hoot owl glasses up the bridge of her nose. "Yes, DICK. Decency in Cannes Kids. How dare they think they can decide what's decent and what isn't."

"I think it was the dildo thing that brought them."

"I wonder where Ruth got all those dildos."

Bridget had a point. Dildos were sort of a one-item purchase. I had never heard of them being sold in bulk. "Ruth's pretty old," I said. "Maybe she's collected them over the years."

"I don't believe in judging a woman's sexuality."

"Me, either," I said, totally judging her sexuality.

Bridget squirmed on the couch, again. "I think my farting labor is back."

"I'll put the fan on."

CHAPTER 9

Sometimes people call me a witch. Sometimes they call me a yenta. Well, not in this town. In Cannes, there are only twelve Jews, so most of the town doesn't know what yenta means. But if they did know what it meant, that's what they would call me. Yenta. Busybody. Well, I'm here to tell you, bubbeleh, you got to be a yenta if you're going to do this job right. You smile, you're nice, you have good manners, and all the time, you're watching and listening and thinking real hard. Because that's our job. We're yenta, the matchmakers.

Lesson 97, Matchmaking advice from your Grandma Zelda

Sand. Sand. Sand. The next evening, I was getting ready for the dinner party, and it was getting harder to avoid my grandmother, who squinted at me every time I was close to her, as if she was trying to see into my brain. I didn't know how long I could hold out. I had to discover quickly if my father was murdered, who murdered him, and why. If it dragged on, my grandmother would find out and suffer from not knowing what happened to her son. I owed it to her to get to the bottom of my father's death and to do it secretly.

"You look nice," my grandmother said, coming into my room. I was wearing a little black dress with black strappy high-heeled sandals. My frizzy hair had been tamed and hung down in long curls. I had dosed my eyelashes with a double batch of mascara, and I was even wearing expensive lipstick that Lucy had given me.

Sand. Sand. Sand. "Thank you, Grandma. We're just going out to a dinner party. You know, grownup couple stuff." *Sand. Sand. Sand.*

Spencer finished tying his tie. "How about me, Zelda? How do I look?"

"You look like fried chicken and mashed potatoes." It was the biggest compliment she could give him. Fried chicken and mashed potatoes were her favorite foods, and she was right. Spencer looked yum-yum. He was perfectly dressed in his perfectly tailored suit. He had been over the moon when I told him that we had been invited to a real dinner party, just like normal, grownup people. He had looked into my eyes with the pride of a man, believing that his woman had decided to be a contented, suburban wife, who liked to dress up and eat chicken breasts with a white sauce.

Poor Spencer. He still didn't realize who he was dealing with.

My grandmother was a different story. She was squinting at me so hard that her nose looked like it had eaten her eyes. I hurried Spencer out of the room and waved goodbye to her with my back turned. *Sand. Sand. Sand.*

It had been a pretty good day. Bridget had had a break from farting labor. DICK and the bubble gum bandits were reasonably quiet. But it was widely believed that they were holding back while they planned their newest attacks to combat the other, and Draco had turned up after school and was a big help to me with inputting matchmaking data into my laptop. I felt good about turning his juvenile delinquent energies into lawful, productive habits. Add to all of that a good hair day and Spencer's fingers dancing up my thigh, as we drove to Roman and Joy's mansion, and I was feeling mighty fine.

"Zelda was right," Spencer told me, driving out of the Historic District. "You look smokin' hot."

"She said I look nice."

"Then, she was wrong. Nice doesn't cut it. You look smokin' hot. Tell me you're not wearing panties."

"I'm wearing the big kind of underpants that come three to a pack and suck my fat into my pancreas."

"Nobody talks dirty like you, Pinky. Nobody."

When we arrived at the mansion, a valet took Spencer's car. "Wow, fancy, Pinky," Spencer said, putting his hand on my lower back. "Is this one of Harry's friends?"

"Uh, sort of."

The truth of the matter was that Spencer was going to

kill me when he found out that I had dredged up my father's past and was spying on his friends because I suspected one of them had killed him after I had seen a suspicious note, even though the police had ruled his death an accident. Spencer wasn't going to be pleased that my foray into being a normal grownup was a total lie. So, other amateur sleuths might have thought I was stupid to bring Spencer with me. I could have brought Lucy and told the suspects that she was my lover, instead of Spencer. But Lucy only had a Taser, and Spencer knew Judo and had a lot of muscles and the ability to arrest whoever he wanted. I would have been more comfortable if he was armed, but, since he was off-duty, he had left his service revolver at home in a safe next to our bed. Still, weighed against each other, Spencer was the wiser choice over Lucy.

But he was going to kill me.

As far as I could tell, we were the last to arrive, except for Rachel Knight, who I hadn't met yet. Joy had pulled out all the stops. There were caterers walking around with trays of champagne and lobster puffs. "Pinky, I'm impressed," Spencer said.

"Gladys," Joy gushed, approaching me. She was wearing a floor-length, print dress and about an inch of pancake makeup. "And who is this handsome man?"

"This is Spencer Bolton," I said.

"Her fiancé," he added.

"Yes, fiancé," I said. It was still weird for me to use titles for my relationships.

"Gladys, you did well," she said, eyeing Spencer and motioning for Roman to come over. When her back was turned, Spencer mouthed *Gladys?* to me. I shrugged. Normally, I wouldn't let anyone get away with calling me by my full name, but sometimes it was just easier not to correct a person over and over.

"Oh, there you are," Roman said, smiling. "Steve, Adam, look who's here!"

Adam and Steve looked pretty much like they did when I had seen them the day before. Adam had moved up from sweatpants to baggy jeans, and thankfully, Steve had left Lady Philomena at home. Steve was happy to see me, but Adam still had the lost look on his face. I introduced everyone to Spencer, and I popped another puff into my mouth.

"We were so happy to have Gladys contact us after so many years," Joy told Spencer.

"She looks a lot like her father, except for the coloring," Roman said.

Spencer arched an eyebrow and pursed his lips. It was clear that he was catching on that this wasn't the dinner party I had sold to him. I side-stepped away from him. "I've been thinking about your insurance," I said to Steve because I was less afraid of a long sales pitch about insurance than I was of Spencer finding out that instead of a contented suburban wife, I was a nosey parker killer hunter.

Steve smiled big. "I thought you would be interested so I prepared a prospectus for you. I've got it in the car. You want me to go get it?"

"After dinner," Joy told him. "Dinner's ready. Shall we?"

The dining room table was decked out in exquisite china. Servers outnumbered the guests two-to-one, and one of them pulled a chair out for me, and tucked it under me when I sat. I could still feel Spencer's eyes on me, but I kept my eyes averted. I could practically hear the cogs in his brain turning.

We were served something I thought was pâté. Roman lifted his glass of wine. "Here's to old friends," he said. "I'm so glad that we're finally all together, again."

Everyone took a sip of their wine, except for Adam. "We're back together when you finally decided we were worthy," he spat and attacked his pâté with his fork.

"That's not fair," Joy said.

"It's sort of fair," Steve said, still sipping his wine.

"So, how do you all know each other?" Spencer asked.

"We used to be friends," Adam told him. "Before Roman became a snooty National Book Award winner."

That was the first time I had heard anything about Roman's success being the impetus for the group's estrangement. Before that moment, they had only spoken about my father's death for the reason they all broke up.

"That's not fair," Joy said.

"It's sort of fair," Steve said.

"Roman has never let his success go to his head," Joy insisted.

"You've got twelve people serving chopped liver, Joy.

To me, that spells success that's gone to his head," Adam said.

"It's pâté from France," she said, obviously insulted.

"So, how do you all know each other?" Spencer asked, again.

All heads turned toward me. "Didn't Gladys tell you?" Steve asked and whistled long and slow.

"They were my father's best friends," I said. My voice was hoarse, and I took a sip of wine.

"You know what?" Spencer said, brightly. "I haven't washed my hands and neither did Gladys. Gladys is very diligent when it comes to personal hygiene. She wouldn't think of eating without washing her hands, first. Isn't that right, Gladys?"

"Well…" I started. Spencer slapped his hand onto mine and gave it a hard squeeze. "I don't want to interrupt dinner," I continued. "but yes, cleanliness is next to godliness, and I'm a big fan of godliness. Love me some godliness. Heaven. Heaven is great. I'm sure hell isn't so bad, either. Probably not a lot of hand-washing in hell, though. But heaven is probably germ-free. Right? I mean there might be those good germs that make mushrooms and yogurt, but not the bad ones that give you diarrhea and make you upchuck. Those are bad germs. So, none of those in heaven next to God. Because God probably doesn't want diarrhea. Come to think of it, why did he create diarrhea? Was that an oversight? Like making the appendix and wisdom teeth? Lots of diarrhea in this world. I guess that means it's not next to godliness. Oh, well. Yes. Diarrhea. What was I talking about?"

Spencer stood and pulled me up by my hand. "We'll be right back," he said and tugged me out of the dining room.

"We don't even know where the bathroom is," I whispered when we left the room. He pushed me into what looked like Roman's office and shoved me up against a wall.

"We're not going to the bathroom, Pinky. That was a ruse about washing our hands so I could speak to you."

"Oh, right. I caught on to that but lost it somewhere." I ran my finger over his lips. "Have I told you how sexy you are tonight?"

"Pinky, if you think seducing me will work, you're right, but first let's talk about what we're doing here."

I put my hands on my hips and stomped my foot on the floor. "My father was murdered, and one of those people in there killed him."

"What do you mean he was murdered? Do you have proof?"

"I have a feeling," I said.

His eyes locked onto mine and didn't let go. "A feeling?"

"A strong feeling, and I found a note." I took it out of my purse and showed it to him.

"This doesn't say much."

"It's a clue."

"Pinky, it's been two months since you last tripped over a dead body. Now you're going back decades to find one because you have Miss Marple withdrawals. I can't help feeling you'll do anything to avoid thinking about our house and wedding."

He was probably right. "I like flooring, but I like sleuthing better."

"What about me? How much do you like me?"

His cocky grin disappeared and so did his ample self-confidence. "You're my best friend."

Spencer's eyes widened. "Really? More than Bridget? More than Lucy?"

"I love Bridget and Lucy, but I can't live without you." I gasped with the weight of my confession. Searching myself, I found that it was true. "But I can live without bamboo flooring and a custom-made couch," I added.

"I'm planning on ravishing you daily on that custom-made couch, Pinky."

"You are?"

"And I plan on watching Padres games, lying on that couch."

"That makes sense."

"Okay. Go ahead and be Miss Marple. It's in your blood to be nosy. You can't push back the tide, and I can't un-nosy Gladie Burger. Or should I say, Gladys?"

"No, you should definitely not say Gladys."

"Let's get back. We've been washing our hands for seven minutes. They must think we're insane germaphobes. They're probably right."

He took my hand and kissed it. We made our way back to the dining room. "And Pinky," Spencer whispered to me. "Ditto. You're my best friend, too. And I probably can't live without you, either. God help me."

When we sat back down at the table, the pâté plates had been removed, and bowls of lobster bisque had been served. I tried to remember not to slurp. The atmosphere had gotten even more icy, but the wine had loosened lips even more.

"I'm sure a guy like you needs insurance," Steve told Roman. "You couldn't call me and throw me some business?"

"I'm sorry, Steve. It didn't occur to me, actually."

Steve dropped his spoon into his bowl. "Of course it didn't. Let's be honest here, okay? You guys never treated me with respect, because my writing was crap and I gave it up. So, now I'm in insurance instead of poetry, and that means you have to forget my name. Am I right?"

"No, of course not," Roman said.

Adam barked laughter. "Yes, he's right. What am I going to talk about with an insurance salesman? You sold out. You're living on a different planet than I am. And Roman is living on his own planet away from all other life forms. Writing one book isn't being a writer, Roman."

"Tell that to Harper Lee," Joy screeched.

The soup bowls were removed and plates of lamb, potatoes, and asparagus were served. It was odd being in such a fancy, mannered environment where everyone was being nasty and hitting below the belt.

"The only good ones among us are dead," Roman said, cutting into his lamb. "Your father was the best," he said to me. "He wouldn't have been trading barbs over a good meal. He would have been discussing the greats in poetry and literature."

"And talking about how lucky we all were to be able to do what we loved," Steve added.

"And cheering us all on," Adam said. "He was our cheerleader. It was impossible to quit when he was around. Even for you, Steve."

"That's true," Steve said. "If he were alive, I would probably still be working on my poetry."

There was silence, while I assumed everyone thought back to their experiences with my father. I felt a surge of jealousy because I couldn't recall many experiences with my father, and we never discussed my talents and what I would do with my life.

"I wonder what Rachel would have thought of us," Joy said after a minute.

"Rachel Knight?" I asked. "Where is she? She couldn't come to dinner tonight?"

"Rachel died, Gladys," Joy said. "She died a year before your father."

"Killed herself," Adam explained. "It was just a matter of time."

"She was on an anti-depressant," Joy told me. "She probably needed a stronger one and more than just medication. She had terrible problems with depression. Isn't that right, Roman?"

Roman put his fork down. "She was a sweet girl. A very sweet girl. It broke my heart when she died. Terrible tragedy. Terrible waste of a sweet girl."

Rachel Knight had died before my father. I hadn't seen that coming. I wondered why my mother had put her on my list. With Rachel Knight dead a year before my father, my suspect list was down to four. There was the weird, Komodo dragon-loving Adam, the jealous insurance salesman Steve, the one-hit literary mogul Roman, and his wife, Joy. My money was on Steve. It made sense that once he killed my father, he was unable to write any longer and hid in the insurance world. But how could I prove that he was the killer?

With the words spoken about the better people who had died before them, the atmosphere had turned less hostile. We finished the main course, and the dessert was served. It was a good meal, and I had eaten so much that my big underpants were cutting off the circulation to my lower body. I was desperate to rip them off, but then my dress wouldn't fit. I took a bite of my dessert. Yum. Chocolate soufflé. Being rich was awesome.

"You must be getting an earful," Joy said to me. "You decided to look up your father's old friends, and you find out that they're very disagreeable. I hope we haven't made you regret your decision."

"Oh, no," I said. "I mean, nobody's perfect and there's nothing to apologize for."

"So, what's your real plan?" Adam asked. "Digging up dirt? Trying to figure out who the real Jonathan Burger was?"

"I don't think Gladie is trying to dig up dirt." Spencer was lying, but I was happy that he was coming to my defense.

"It was hard to accept Jonathan's death," Roman said. "But in the end, there was nothing romantic about it. No mystery at all about it. It was just a tragedy, and like most tragedies, it was banal. Mundane. He lost control of his motorcycle, and his life was snuffed out. I'm sorry that we couldn't give you more information than that."

"True," Spencer said. "It was sort of mundane. He had traveled that piece of road on his motorcycle hundreds of times. Perhaps thousands of times. But for some reason on that day, on that day with perfect weather and perfect driving conditions, he lost control of his bike, and he had an accident so bad that he died. Mundane. Banal. A slip of the wheel. Taking the turn too sharply. Going five miles faster than he normally drove. Simple, small mistakes leading to a deadly consequence. Who knows? Maybe we'll never know."

"But Gladys wants to know?" Adam asked. "Is that why we're here?"

"Maybe we're here because we all want to know," Steve said. "After all, we never talked about that day. We never even went to the funeral."

Only my grandmother, my mother, and I went to the funeral. Grandma had wanted it that way. The grief was too private to share.

"You can't make sense out of the senseless," Joy said, wisely.

Without answers, the table went quiet, again. I wasn't getting anywhere except that my mourning for my father had cracked wide open, and inside me, I was yelling at the universe for taking my father in such a senseless, stupid accident.

"So, who's richer?" Steve asked after a long silence, changing the subject. "Roman or Adam? Roman gets all the press and the awards, and Adam is a mountain man recluse, but I bet it's Adam. How about it, Adam? You richer than Roman? How many of those children's books have you published?"

"Sixty-two."

"Sixty-two books?" Spencer asked, impressed. "You've written sixty-two books?"

"I like to write," Adam said.

"What do you write? Maybe I've read it," Spencer said.

"Nah, you look like you're strictly a Patterson reader," Adam said. He was right. Spencer loved James Patterson. "I write middle-grade books."

"That's for eight-to-twelve year olds," Joy explained. "Adam is a star in the middle grade market. He's been on the New York Times bestseller list for ten years without a break."

"Eleven years," Adam said, talking to his dessert.

"Roman went the National Book Award route, and Adam went the fart jokes route," Steve said. "I'm trying to figure out if there's more money in prestigious awards or farts."

"Probably farts," Roman said, laughing.

"Farts?" I asked.

"*Fart Boy*," Adam said. "That's the name of my series.

The Adventures of Fart Boy."

CHAPTER 10

Some people are thinkers, and some people are doers. You're a Burger, and Burger women are both. We're thinking and doing. Doing and thinking. It's called shpilkes, and we got it bad. Our shpilkes keep us moving, going forward. Sometimes the shpilkes make us a little heavier on the doing than we are on the thinking, and we find ourselves in the middle of a mess without having a plan on how to get out of it. Don't worry about it, dolly. Let your shpilkes free. If you find yourself in a mess, you'll get out of it, eventually.

Lesson 134, Matchmaking advice from your Grandma Zelda

"What did you say?" I asked.

"About what?" Adam asked.

"Your series. What's it called?"

"*Fart Boy*?"

"Yes, that's it. *Fart Boy.*"

I almost lunged over the table and strangled Adam Mancuso to death. *Fart Boy* was my father's idea. I had read it in his box in my grandmother's attic. It was all clear to me, now. Adam had stolen the idea for *Fart Boy* from my father and had murdered him. Now, he was a rich and famous author, and my father was dead.

I was fuming. I was sitting across from the man with my father's blood on his hands. No matter what, I was going to take the bastard down.

Spencer leaned over and whispered in my ear. "Are you okay? Your face is red, and you're panting like a Chihuahua."

"I'm fine."

After dinner, there was brandy and cigars, but I needed to get out of there fast. I took Joy aside. "Thank you so much for your hospitality. It means a lot to me." I took her hand in mine and gave her my best earnest look. "My Aunt Flow has come to visit," I told her. "So, I need to leave. I hate to eat and run like this."

"Oh, no, dear, I totally understand."

Truth be told my Aunt Flow was always some light spotting for three days and had never stopped me from doing a thing. Besides, I wasn't expecting it for another ten days, but it was a great excuse, and it worked. Spencer and I said our goodbyes, and Adam and Steve stayed behind to continue their visit.

We got Spencer's car back from the valet, and we

drove away. "That must have been hard for you, Pinky. I'm so sorry," Spencer said as he drove.

"It's okay. I want to make a quick stop on the way home. Make a left at the bottom of the hill."

"I know you were looking for answers, and you got none."

"Yeah, no answers. That was hard." I didn't think it would be a good idea to let him know about *Fart Boy* just yet. I had a plan, and I didn't want him nixing it.

"You know, family is important. I get that. And I know you want closure. That nightmare of a dinner didn't give you any. Do you want to talk about it?"

"Yeah, sure. Talk about it."

"Okay, Pinky. It's going to be hard to let this go. Crazy accidents are the hardest to accept. I agree that any of those people could kill a person, but in this case, it's obvious that you're going to just have to swallow your grief and let it evaporate with time."

"You're right. You're right. Evaporate. Time. Turn here."

Spencer turned. "And I don't think you should have anything to do with those people, anymore. I think there's a reason Zelda wasn't in touch with them and a reason they had gone their separate ways."

"True. True. A reason. Turn right at the second street."

"At least they said your father was a great guy. That's something, right?" Spencer said.

"Yeah, that was really good. Here you go. Turn here."

Spencer turned onto the dirt road. Spencer flipped on the car's bright lights because there was no street light, and it was pitch black. "Pinky, where are we going? I thought you needed tampons."

"My period's not for another ten days. Okay, slow down. We're almost there."

"Where?"

"His house."

"Whose house?"

"Pay attention, Spencer!"

"Pinky, help me out, here. Where are we?"

The house came into view. I pointed to a stand of trees. "Park behind the trees so he doesn't see us."

"Who doesn't see us?"

"This is serious, Spencer. Park behind the trees."

Miraculously, he listened to me and parked behind the trees and turned off the car and the lights. Spencer turned toward me in his seat. "Okay. Cough it up, Pinky. What's happening?"

"Listen, you're either with me or against me."

"What am I? Al Qaeda?"

I wagged my finger at him. "Here's what we're going to do. We're going to break into the house and find the proof that he's the killer."

"Who's the killer?"

"Haven't you been paying attention?"

Spencer grabbed me and pulled me toward him,

planting a deep kiss on my mouth. The world spun around, and I got dizzy. Spencer's tongue did magical work, and I melted against him. When I finally relaxed, he broke off the kiss.

"Pinky, where are we?"

"Adam Mancuso's house. He killed my father."

I told him about *Fart Boy*. Spencer said it wasn't proof of anything, but I could tell that he was interested.

"I can't break into a house, Pinky. I'm the Chief of Police. I would need a warrant, and no judge—no matter how stoned or drunk he may be—would give me a warrant on the basis of finding pages of *Fart Boy* in a box in your attic."

"That's what I figured," I said. "That's why I'm going to break in myself, and you're going to stay out here and be the lookout. I figure if he smokes a cigar with his brandy, we've got a thirty-minute head start in front of Adam."

"I'm the Chief of Police."

"Yes, I know. So you know how to be a lookout."

"No. I mean, yes I know how, but I'm not going to be an accessory to breaking and entering. I'm the Chief of Police, Pinky."

"You keep saying that, like you're bragging about it, but you being the Chief of Police has been a huge pain in the ass for me."

Even in the dark car, I could see Spencer's eyes grow wide. "Are you kidding me? You're damned lucky I'm the Chief. Any other guy would have put your ass in jail months ago. If it weren't for me, you'd be wearing orange and eating your meals with a spork."

He was probably right. "You're wrong, Spencer. Totally wrong. Let me go in. I know the evidence is in that house of horrors, and I'm going to get it. Time is ticking away."

I opened the car door, but before I could step out, car lights approached us. I closed the door quickly and watched through the window at what I assumed was Adam's car driving down the dirt road right at us.

"He must not have smoked the cigar. Good thing we're hiding behind the trees," I said.

Spencer sighed. "Why couldn't I have fallen for Jessica Fieldstone, like my mother wanted? But no, I had to fall for a nuclear explosion with great legs."

"Shh. He's getting out of his car. You think I have great legs? Sh! Never mind that now."

I watched Adam march into his house. The cabin lit up as he turned on the lights, but I couldn't see what he was doing from our vantage point in the car.

"Look what you did," I complained. "You wasted my time, and I couldn't go in and investigate."

"If I had let you, he would have come home while you were sifting through his desk."

He was right. I wouldn't have had enough time to find the proof that he had stolen *Fart Boy* and killed my father.

"He's probably in for the night," Spencer said.

"I think you're right."

"Thank God. The madwoman shows some sanity."

I opened the door. "So, I'll just have to go in and confront him."

Spencer reached around me and pulled the door closed. "Not so fast. You're not going in there."

"You're right. He might go out, later to get ice cream or whatever. We should watch his house for a while and maybe I'll get another shot at it."

"Fine," Spencer said, locking the doors. "It's not much, but I'll take it for now."

About two minutes later, we both fell fast asleep. Later, I would blame the heavy meal and the wine. It was also the dark, quiet car, and the soft sound of Spencer's breathing. In any case, we dropped like stones for about twenty minutes. I didn't wake up until Spencer jingled his keys, when he had woken and was about to start the car and drive away.

I slapped my hand over his. "No way. We're not going anywhere. I'm going in."

Before Spencer could stop me, I opened the door and ran out. I heard Spencer come after me, but even in the dark and in high heels, I ran fast, and I got to the front door and knocked before Spencer could stop me.

"Great," he grumbled. "You did it. You knocked on the door." There was a rustling behind us. "What the hell is that?" Spencer asked, looking into the dark, alarmed.

"Probably the porcupine," I said.

"The what?"

"Adam has a collection of dangerous animals." I knocked, again, and this time the door opened slowly, creaking loudly. "Look at that. He didn't close his door. Hello? Adam?" I called.

"I don't like this," Spencer said.

"Adam? It's Gladie with Spencer. We came to say, hello."

Nothing. No response. Not a noise. I took a step inside. "Mr. Mancuso, this is Chief of Police, Spencer Bolton," Spencer called, loudly. "I'm concerned about your safety, and I'm coming into the house."

Still nothing. I took another step, but Spencer yanked me back, pulling me behind him. "You stay here. Do you hear me, Pinky? You stay here."

"Okay," I lied.

We walked through the living room. It didn't look any different than it had when I had been there before, except there was a bowl and spoon on an end table next to the couch.

"See?" I whispered to Spencer. "He did eat ice cream."

"So, where is he now?"

"Maybe he got eaten by his Komodo dragon."

"His what?"

"Or he's lying in wait for us, poised to kill us in a terrible way."

"Let's go back to the Komodo dragon thing," Spencer said.

"Do you hear that?" There was a buzzing sound, and I

followed it into the kitchen. The noise turned out to be the aquarium. I watched the fish swim around, and I got a creepy feeling up my spine.

"Nice aquarium," Spencer said.

"They're piranhas."

"What the hell?"

We stared at the fish swimming, and as if on cue, we searched the bottom of the tank at the same time, looking for human body parts. There was nothing. Not even a shoe. Or a finger.

"I'm creeped out, Pinky."

"Maybe he really did get eaten by his dragon. Either that or some other scary pet that he has. I didn't have the chance to see the whole house. He could have a whole zoo's worth of scary pets. I guess we'll have to do the search now. Let's start in the office."

I was still determined to find proof that Adam stole my father's work and killed him. I didn't know if he had gone out for a walk or whatever, and I didn't care if he discovered me snooping. I wanted to confront him. I wanted answers immediately. I wanted to find out the truth and bring Adam to justice.

We found the office without much difficulty, and as soon as Spencer opened the door, we discovered where Adam kept his pet dragon.

Spencer screamed like a little girl. I didn't scream. Instead, I jumped onto Spencer's back and held on for dear life. "What kind of crazy person has a Komodo dragon in his house?" Spencer screeched, his voice a couple octaves higher than normal. He sounded like he was selling Girl Scout cookies. The dragon seemed to be attracted to Spencer's high-pitched scream. He came right at him.

"Why didn't I bring a gun?" Spencer screamed, again. He backed up, while I held on tight to him, my legs wrapped around his waist and my hands around his throat. Spencer made a beeline for the back of the house, outrunning the dragon. We hid behind a door, and through the crack between the door and the wall, we watched as the dragon lost interest in eating Spencer and walked creepily on his reptile legs toward the front door and out into the wild.

"Maybe he isn't hungry because he already ate Adam," I whispered in Spencer's ear. "Adam was pretty big, and he had a stomach full of food."

"What else is in this house of horrors?" Spencer whispered back.

I climbed off Spencer's back. "At least the office is clear, now. Let's go check it out."

Spencer looked like there was no way he was going to go into the office, in case the dragon returned or there was a second one hiding somewhere, but he decided to go in because he had to search for Adam remnants. I didn't care about Adam remnants. I was looking for paper.

Boy, did I find a lot of paper. Adam was a pack rat. The walls were lined with filing cabinets, which were bursting at the seams with paper, and boxes of paper covered most of the floor. It would take days, if not weeks, to search through all of it. I didn't care.

I started by looking through the filing cabinets, first under B for Burger and then J for Jonathan. Eureka. There were a series of notes from my father to Adam. I started reading.

"What did you find?" Spencer asked.

He took a couple of the notes and started to read, too. "My father was helping him, critiquing his work." I read out loud. "*I love your Fart Boy idea, Adam. Please don't quit. Have faith in your abilities and your creativity. You have something special to offer the world. Your friend, Jonathan.*"

Spencer put his arm around me. "So, I guess this means that he didn't steal the idea."

"No. I was wrong."

"Hold on, let me record that." He took his phone out of his blazer pocket.

"Ha. Ha. Nice try. I'm not saying it, again."

We searched through the entire house. We found a few snakes and a spider collection. Adam was gross, but he probably wasn't a killer.

But he was missing.

"I don't know if I should call this in or what," Spencer said. "My gut tells me to leave and come back in the morning. He'll probably turn up at some point."

"And you can look for the dragon easier in the daylight."

Spencer ran a hand over his face. "Oh, Jesus. I forgot about the dragon. We'll have to drag the lake for him. Block off the park. What a nightmare."

I belched. "I've got terrible heartburn. Rich people's food doesn't agree with me. I wonder if he has a soda. That would hit the spot."

"Fine. Let's get you a soda, and I'll call in about the dragon."

We went back into the kitchen. Spencer turned his back to me, leaned against the counter, and dialed Remington's phone. I opened the refrigerator.

"Um," I said.

"Give me a soda, too," Spencer said, focusing on his phone.

"Um."

"Remington's not answering. He's supposed to be on call."

"Um."

"Maybe Margie's up."

"Um."

"I can only imagine what DICK is going to say about me letting a dragon loose on the town," Spencer complained. "Maybe it'll eat a few DICK members and then I won't have to worry about them. DICK members. Ha! DICK members...Get it? Margie's not answering, either. Any kind of soda would be good, Pinky. I guess rich people's food doesn't agree with me, either."

"I don't think we want his soda," I said. "I think we should wait and get soda at home."

"I've got wicked heartburn. I don't think Adam

would be upset if I took a can of Coke."

"I don't think he'll be upset, either…I mean, not anymore…but his refrigerator isn't very hygienic."

"Pinky, I'm a guy. You should see the fridge at the station."

"I think this fridge is worse," I said.

Spencer finally turned around and got an eyeful of the fridge. "Holy shit."

"Holy shit. Yes, those are the words I was looking for. Holy shit. Holy shit!" I took a deep breath. "Holy shit! Holy shit! Holy shit!"

"He's a big man," Spencer said. "Amazing how he fits in there. These French door refrigerators sure are roomy."

Adam Mancuso, successful middle grade author of *The Adventures of Fart Boy,* was stuffed into his refrigerator, obviously stabbed repeatedly, his blood was splattered over his food, including a six-pack of Diet Coke, which I was definitely not going to drink.

CHAPTER 11

Sometimes your match will just not be ready. Ready for a human, I mean. He may be a little backward, a little socially awkward, or he might just not have had any experience with relationships or familial love. He's not ready. In some of these cases, your match needs a substitute, someone to shower his love on as practice for the real thing. I'm talking about a pet. A four-legged something, furry or not, that he can learn to love. Once he has experience with a pet, he can graduate to a person. Pets are really helpful to matchmakers, bubbeleh.

Lesson 139, Matchmaking advice from your Grandma Zelda

Surprisingly, the word of a dead, stabbed man stuffed into a refrigerator didn't cause a stir, but the word of an escaped Komodo dragon had spread like wildfire. It turned out to be the most interesting to grocery store tabloids, who drove into Cannes within an hour of the dragon's escape to write about every aspect of the story. It didn't take them long to find Adam's house because Spencer's men had surrounded it with flood lights, and it was now the brightest area of Cannes, that late at night.

I sat in the back of Remington's car, while outside, Spencer barked orders at his men and fended off the media.

"I have no idea if a Komodo dragon can impregnate a woman. What kind of question is that?" I heard Spencer growl at reporters. "No, it's not Alien or Predator. It's just a reptile. No, I'm pretty sure it can't fly. What do you mean, did it have access to automatic weapons? It's a big, ugly lizard!"

It went on for a couple hours with no sign of the dragon. Animal control called in more animal control from San Diego, and the media stuck around, excited to prepare a slew of salacious stories about a children's author and his possibly kinky lifestyle with dragons.

By the time that Margie drove me away to my grandmother's house, DICK had shown up at Adam's house, joining the media and the other looky-loos, ready to battle what they figured had to be a total lack of decency.

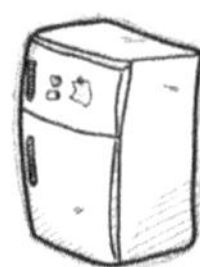

I slept like death, like poor Adam Mancuso stuffed into his refrigerator. I woke up in bed in the fetal position with a pillow full of drool after a disturbing dream where I was Khaleesi, and I was trying to ride a Komodo dragon, which instead of breathing fire, was trying to bite my foot off.

When I woke up, instead of Spencer in bed with me, my grandmother was sitting on the edge of the bed, watching me sleep. She was wearing her blue housecoat and plastic slip-on slippers. "Hi, Grandma," I said, wiping my mouth.

"There's a dragon in town."

"I know," I said.

"The DICK people say it's a sign that we're not decent, and they're going to take it up a notch. It's going to be hard for Meryl. Can you go to her library today and give her moral support?"

"Sure. No problem. Have you seen Spencer?"

"He didn't come home last night. Between the bubble gum and the dragon, he has his hands full."

I nodded. Grandma was quiet, which wasn't a normal state for her. "Nice day," I said.

"It's going to be sunny and seventy-five degrees with a slight breeze. Not a lot of humidity for the dragon."

"Do you know where it is?"

"I know love, dolly, not reptiles." I nodded. I could feel her studying me, and I tried to think of sand, but I was too tired. "I'm going to bed today."

I sat up. "You are? Is it your heart? Should I call the doctor?"

"It is my heart, but not like you think."

Heartache. It was my fault. I had stirred up old

wounds about loss and grief. "You know about Adam Mancuso?"

Grandma put her hand on my arm and rubbed it. "You have the Gift, dolly. You know things that I'll never know. I'm counting on you."

"On me?" The idea that anyone would count on me for anything important sent waves of panic running through my body. What if I let her down? She might never recover.

"On you, bubbeleh. I have confidence in you. I trust you." I looked in her eyes, and I knew she wasn't lying, but there was a fifty-percent chance she was crazy. Why else would she have confidence in me? I mean, I let a dragon loose on the town. I couldn't be trusted! "I'll get out of bed when you find out the truth."

I followed her to her room and tucked her into bed. I handed her the remote, and I went downstairs to make her breakfast. The doorbell rang, and I answered it. Bridget was standing on the porch, wearing a red muumuu, which along with her blue eye shadow, made her look a little like the American flag.

"This baby is never going to be born," she said. "What's the gestation of an elephant? I think I'm giving birth to an elephant."

Her belly looked like she was going to give birth to an elephant, but I didn't think she wanted to hear that. "No, you're not going to give birth to an elephant. You're giving birth to a sweet, baby boy. I saw the ultrasound."

"Fake news, Gladie. Fake news. Do you have food?

I'll eat anything with hot sauce. I heard hot sauce induces labor."

I made toasted bagels with cream cheese and raspberry jam, coffee, and sliced cantaloupe so our insides wouldn't turn into toxic sludge. Bridget and I brought the breakfasts upstairs to keep my grandmother company while we all ate.

The TV was on to national news. "Oh my God, look," Bridget said, pointing. "They're talking about us!"

My grandmother turned up the sound on the television. They were showing Adam's house, but instead of focusing on him being murdered and stuffed into his refrigerator next to leftover deli, they were all about the Komodo dragon, which had been sighted in every nook and cranny in town with hysterical calls to law enforcement breaking all records.

"This is worse than the circus tiger incident of 1972," Grandma said.

"Look! There's Ruth!" Bridget announced, pointing at the TV.

"If you're not going to buy tea, you can go straight to hell," she yelled at the press pool in town, who had stopped by Tea Time for local color. "I don't care about dragons or gryphons or elves or leprechauns. This is a place of business, you soul-sucking vultures, cadaver-eating, gore-chasing, lowlife bottom-feeders!"

"Wow, Ruth knows a lot of adjectives," Bridget said.

"What do you say about DICK's assertions that you are a prime cause of the indecency sweeping through this town?" a reporter asked Ruth on television.

I couldn't make out the answer because the station beeped through all of it. My grandmother muted the television, took a bite of her bagel, and washed it down with coffee.

"Today's going to be stressful," Grandma said. "I'm sorry that I can't help, but I'll be in bed all day."

"I'm glad it'll be stressful," Bridget said, pushing her glasses up the bridge of her nose. "Stress causes labor."

Wow, a lot of things caused labor.

"Don't forget Meryl," my grandmother told me. She yawned, and I took her plate and cup from her and brought it downstairs, where I cleaned up.

"What's going on with Meryl?" Bridget asked.

"I don't know. I just know we're supposed to go to her library and give her moral support."

"I can do that," Bridget said.

The doorbell rang, and I answered it. It was Draco, and he was carrying an armful of license plates. "Hi. School's closed on account of a runaway dragon. I thought I could get some of that work done and you could feed me."

"What are the license plates for?"

"Phase Three in the resistance against DICK."

"Okay." I thought it best not to ask for details.

In the attic, I handed Draco a box of Pop-Tarts, a bag of Doritos, and a can of cream soda. I showed him where to start with his computer stuff. It was a bunch of tedious data entry. "I'll be back in a couple hours. If you need anything, ask my grandmother in her bedroom. It might be good for you to check on her, anyway."

Draco put his license plates down in the corner of the attic. "Sure thing," he said.

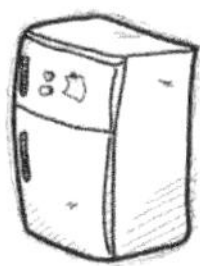

Bridget drove us to the library in her VW Bug. "What's going on with Zelda?" she asked. "Why is she in bed? Is she having a blind day?"

Every once in a while, my grandmother had a blind day, when her third eye couldn't see, and she would become distraught and disoriented. On those days, she would mostly stay in bed.

"No, she's in bed because of me." Because I stirred up painful memories of her son's death.

"I can't believe that's true, Gladie." Bridget patted my knee. "When you moved into town, Zelda got a new lease on life. I've never seen her so happy."

It never dawned on me that my presence actually did something for her. I thought the benefits to us living together were totally one-sided. I got a place to live and food in my mouth, a support system, and training for a new profession, but my grandmother only got more responsibility and stress. Could Bridget be right, and I actually brought something to the equation?

I opened my window and let the wind blow on my

face. My grandmother was right about the weather. The air was clean and refreshing, and the sun was out. But the town was a mess. Television vans lined Main Street, and journalists were interviewing cardigan-wearing DICK members, who were giving them stories about how indecent we were.

As we drove by, I saw the mayor, jumping up and down behind a couple of them, shouting, "It's not true! It's not true! We're small-town America! We have sixteen pie shops in town!"

"It looks like the mayor's about to go into labor," I told Bridget.

"I can see the vein popping out on his forehead from here. I feel bad because I should be front and center in this fight against DICK, but my sandwich board doesn't fit me anymore, and my heart's not in it. Do you think I'll want to protest again, once the baby's born?"

"I can't imagine you going very long without protesting labor infractions or the patriarchy. You're probably just retaining fluid, and that's why you don't want to protest."

"I had to squeeze my feet into my flip-flops to get them on. If you stick me with a hat pin, I'll leak all over. I could fill a pool."

The library was buzzing with activity. There were several DICK people outside with their hands up in the air, shouting something and more or less blocking the entrance. Bridget parked in back, and we went inside, avoiding the DICK line.

"Fascists," Bridget muttered. "Nazi, jack-booted, puritans. If I wasn't bearing life, and I didn't have hemorrhoids, I would give them a piece of my mind."

Inside the library, Meryl was chasing after several DICK people. She was apoplectic and whispering as loudly as she could, chastising them for whatever they were doing.

"What are they doing?" I asked Bridget.

She gasped. "They're armed with Sharpies, Gladie. Black Sharpies."

We joined Meryl and watched as a DICK man opened a book and began to run through offending printed words with his black Sharpie. "He wrote in a library book," I whispered to Bridget, aghast. "The library police are going to get him." When I was six years old, Meryl had cornered me in my bedroom, demanding my overdue copy of *Johnny Tremain*. I shuddered to think what she would do to someone for defacing a book.

"What do you think you're doing? Stop! Stop!" Meryl whispered to them.

It was no use. They were an army of Sharpies, and they were taking no prisoners. The gang of DICK people were Sharpieing books, left and right. "Bad words, bad thoughts, bad images," the man said.

Meryl's face turned red. "You can't do that," she whispered as loudly as she could. "Help! Police!"

"I'll call the police," I said.

"They won't come," Meryl said, frantically. "They're hunting the dragon. They say they can't be bothered with genre fiction."

"Nazis!" Bridget shouted at the top of her lungs. "Book burners!"

"We're not burning books. We're censoring them. There's a big difference," the man announced.

Bridget adjusted her glasses and blew out a ton of indignant air. The pre-pregnant Bridget that I had known was back. I recognized the rage of a free-speech activist when faced with a cardigan-wearing man armed with a Sharpie in a library. "To arms! To arms! Townspeople, attack! We are being overrun by fascist book burners! They may take our lives, but they'll never take our freedom!"

With impressive speed, considering Bridget's girth, she grabbed a hardback copy of Michener's *Hawaii* and laid one on the DICK man's head. He flew back and took down the historical fiction shelves with him.

"The Dewey Decimal system!" Meryl yelled, forgetting to whisper.

The DICK man regained his balance and raised his hand to Bridget. "Don't you dare!" she yelled. Her voice came out in a loud bellow, like the voice of God in a movie about the Ten Commandments. "I am bearing life!"

He put his hand down. His eyes darted from right to left, perhaps flummoxed about what he should do when faced with a pissed off, very pregnant woman.

The DICK members gathered around him to support their man, but the townspeople gathered behind Bridget. "Power to the people, motherfucker!" she yelled, which drew gasps from the cardigans.

But it worked. With one imperious finger, pointed at the exit and a bark of "Get out!" in Meryl's best librarian's imperious tone, the DICK people left with their Sharpies.

After they were gone, Meryl slumped onto a wooden chair and laid her head on the table. I sat next to her and patted her back. The assistant librarian counted up the damage. There were twelve books that had been Sharpied. Not too bad, considering.

"You were very brave, Meryl," I told her.

"The thing is, Gladie, that I liked DICK before all of this. I was rooting for them against the bubble gum bandits." She lifted her head off the table. "I've been scraping bubble gum off every surface in the library, you know. Pounds of bubble gum, Gladie. But the bubble gum bandits never touched the books. They had respect for the written word. Not like those DICK people. Those DICK people are dicks, Gladie."

Bridget stood over us in a Wonder Woman pose. "I'm feeling great," she said. "My feet even de-swelled a little."

My phone rang. It was Lucy, and I answered. "You found the weird animal man in his refrigerator?" she demanded.

"I'm sorry."

"You never wait for me. I'm never there for the big action."

"There's still a dragon on the loose. Maybe you'll stumble over it."

"I need more information," she insisted. "Come here for lunch."

"We just ate."

"I could eat, again," Bridget said.

"Come over," Lucy said. "Harry invited a chef from Italy to feed us."

"Okay. We'll be right over."

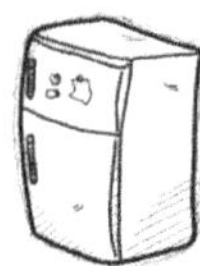

Lucy must have been watching out her front window because she opened the front door before I had the chance to ring the bell. "There you are," she said, breathlessly. "Come in. Quick."

A couple months ago, Lucy had married a man I called Uncle Harry, even though we weren't related. They had both sold their mansions to buy an even bigger mansion. It dawned on me that I could have moved in with them, and they wouldn't have even known. It looked like the Czar of Russia lived there.

"Hey there, Legs," Uncle Harry called to me. He was sitting at the table in the dining room. A big television was on, playing a boxing match, and Harry's attention moved between us, his food, and the fight at regular intervals.

"Hi, Uncle Harry. How's tricks?"

"I lost three-thousand at my poker game this week. Lousy luck. Where's the cop? I like when he joins my game.

He gives me good luck."

"He's been busy, building his house. And now, he's trying to slay a dragon."

"His house? Don't you mean your house?"

"Yeah, sure," I said.

"Do you mind if I put my feet up when I eat?" Bridget asked. She sat down sideways on a chair and put her feet up on the chair next to her.

"Lucy sat at the head of the table, across from Harry, and she motioned for me to sit on her right.

"What the hell happened?" she asked me.

"Today, I'm so happy to have such wonderful people to serve," the Italian chef said, appearing in the dining room in his chef's coat and hat. "For lunch, I have prepared melon with prosciutto, carbonara, salmon with--how do you say--potatoes, and for dessert, tiramisu and coffee."

"Sounds great," Harry announced and went back to watching the fight.

"I like me some pasta," Bridget said.

The chef left the room, and Lucy asked me again to tell her what happened the night before. I told her about the dinner party and about *Fart Boy.*

"I can relate to that title," Bridget said.

Lucy gasped. "So, Adam did it. He stole your daddy's idea and killed him."

The chef served the melon, and we dug in. "That's what I thought," I told Lucy with my mouth full. "That's why we broke into Adam's house after dinner."

"You broke in?"

"Well, the door was open." I explained about Adam coming home and about Spencer and me falling asleep.

"And you found him in the refrigerator," Lucy breathed.

I nodded. "After I let the dragon loose."

"I heard that that dragon spit poison juices at some old lady's dog, and melted the pooch into the ground," Uncle Harry said and finished his melon.

"Where did you hear that?" Lucy asked.

"It was on that entertainment show before the fights."

"So, who did it?" Lucy asked me, returning to the topic of Adam's murder.

"I don't know."

The chef took our plates and came back with the carbonara.

"I guess it had to be a man," Lucy continued. "I mean, someone strong enough to stuff him into the refrigerator."

"I resent you stereotyping along gender lines," Bridget said. "This carbonara is awesome. Is there enough for seconds?"

"I guess a woman could have done it," Lucy said, considering it. "If she ate keto and did weights or something."

Bridget wagged her fork at Lucy. "Or Pilates. That stuff is hard."

My cellphone rang, and I answered it. "Pinky, oh my God. Oh my God!"

"What?" I asked, panicked. Spencer was on the other line, and he sounded terrified.

"The dragon!"

CHAPTER 12

Love is a process. Just like baking a cake. Of course, I have no idea how to bake a cake, but I'll bet dollars to doughnuts that there are steps. So, love is a process. There are steps, but the steps are not the same size and not the same difficulty, and you never know when one is going to show up. In other words, dolly, there are no rules to the process. Confused? Don't worry. The important thing is that you prepare your matches not to want everything at once and accept one step after another until love is there for as long as she lives.

Lesson 45, Matchmaking advice from your Grandma Zelda

"Spencer? Are you okay?"

"It treed me! I'm treed!"

"What does that mean?"

"I wanted to tell you, in case, ohhhhh eowah!"

"Eowah? What does that mean? Spencer? Spencer?" I looked at the phone. He had disconnected. "He hung up."

"Is he investigating the murder?" Lucy asked.

"I don't think so. I think he's working on the dragon thing."

"Tell him to be careful of its poison spit juices," Uncle Harry said, focusing on the fight on TV.

"I wonder if I should go help him," I said and then Lucy, Bridget, and I broke out into laughter. There was no way I could help Spencer with a dragon. I would probably wind up getting him eaten.

"Oh, Gladie, you're such a card," Lucy said. "So, what's next in the investigation?"

"I need to get back into that house and look for clues," I heard myself say and then had doubts. "Do you think they cleaned out his poisonous spider collection?"

"I don't know," Lucy said. "I heard they have every animal control person in Southern California going after the dragon. Maybe they don't have anyone to spare for the spiders."

Ugh. I hated spiders even more than I hated giant lizards.

"Why do you think he was murdered?" Lucy asked me.

"I think he knew who murdered my father. And now the suspects are down to three."

Lucy didn't care about poisonous spiders if it meant she wouldn't miss any excitement. I tried to explain to her that I wasn't expecting any more excitement, but she didn't believe me. So, since I had to get back home and pay Draco, she insisted that she would meet me there in an hour before I returned to Adam's house to break into his office, again.

Bridget drove me home. Hitting a fascist with a hardback book had made her feel a lot better about being pregnant, and after she dropped me off, she was content to go home alone and take a nap.

Grandma's house was quiet. With her out of commission in bed, and the town's groups, committees, and volunteering in a deep drought, for the first time ever, my grandmother's house wasn't the center of activity in town. It was sad and abnormal, and it made me disoriented, like my reality had shifted and everything I had ever known to be true turned out to be false.

Checking on my grandmother, I found her asleep with the television on to an infomercial. I turned off the TV and made sure she was still breathing. Yep, she was okay.

I tiptoed out and shut her door with a soft click. Then, I climbed up to the attic. Draco was sitting at the folding table, tapping the keys on my laptop with a stack of my grandmother's index cards next to him. The Doritos bag and Pop-Tarts box were empty, and I was guessing he had finished the cream soda, too. I had expected him to be reading comic books or whatever young people did, but Draco surprised me by working diligently.

"These are some trippy cards," he said when I entered.

"Matchmaking isn't for the faint of heart."

"People sure don't want to be alone," he said, wisely.

"Love is a powerful drug."

He shrugged. "I'd rather play Grand Theft Auto."

"Most guys would. Can you come back tomorrow after school? I'll get more junk food."

"Sure. I'll come after school or earlier if the dragon is still on the loose. I forgot to check on your grandma."

"That's okay. She's fine."

The doorbell rang. "I'm going to get that," I said.

"I'll turn off the laptop and be down there in a sec."

Downstairs, I opened the front door. A guy with a flattened nose and big, cauliflower ears was standing on the porch. "I'm here for the plates," he said. His voice was low and gravely.

"What plates?"

"You know, lady. The plates. C'mon. Hand 'em over."

"I don't know what plates you're talking about. We're using all our plates. We don't have any to give away."

The man scrunched up his face. "I got a call to come here to get the plates. I don't got all day, you know. I'm going to be driving for hours, and if I don't have the plates, I can't do the driving."

"You have to drive with plates?" I asked, confused. "Like a circus act thing?"

Draco came barreling down the stairs. "Hey, man," he said. "Here I am."

He handed the big guy his armful of license plates. "Oh, phase three," I said, remembering. "Do I want to know what phase three is?"

"It's genius," Draco said and walked out with the goon.

As they left, Lucy drove up the driveway and opened her window. "What's going on?" she called from her car. "Did I miss anything?"

"Nope. Nobody's dead."

"Oh, good. Come on and get in the car. Time's a wasting."

I grabbed my purse and got in her car. I was in a hurry, too. I needed to get answers on the double so that Grandma could get out of bed, and our lives could go back to normal, whatever that was.

Across the street, the construction workers were sitting on the front lawn, soaking up the rays. With Spencer busy with DICK and the dragon, he didn't have time to be on top of the workers to actually work and finish the house on time. If I couldn't save him from the dragon, the least I could do was fill in for Spencer with the workers. Uncle Harry's comment about it being my house, too, really hit home. I urged Lucy to stop the car in front of the house, and

I stepped onto the sidewalk.

"Hello," I called to the men. "It's me. Gladie. I'm with Spencer, you know. And this is his house. I mean, this is my house. Mine! And well, how's the work going? You're working, right?"

"Yep," a couple men responded.

"Don't you worry," another man said. "We've got this under control."

They went back to lying down in the sun. "All righty, then," I said. "I mean, if you're doing what you're supposed to be doing, that's great."

Lucy's car door slammed behind me, and I heard the click-clack of her heels on the pavement. "Hey, pretty lady," one of the men said to her.

"Listen up, you egg-sucking dogs," she announced in her thick Southern drawl. "I know what you good-for-nothing, pack of no-accounts, about as useful as a steering wheel on a mule, think you're doing. But there's a tree stump in Louisiana with a higher IQ then y'all, if you think that just because Mr. Bolton is busy you can loll around here all day and get your asses paid. You can butter your butts and call them biscuits, but that doesn't make it true. So, get your smelly selves that could gag a maggot up and get to work, or I'm gonna jerk a knot in your tail, so help me Jesus. Are we clear?"

They were clear. They jumped up and ran into the house. Lucy stuck her finger in the air, signaling me to wait a second, and sure enough, the sound of hammering and sawing began. She smoothed her dress and nodded.

"They think they can do what they want, just because we're women," she muttered. "Well, they can keep it up and watch me cancel their birth certificates."

"That's right," I said, because I couldn't think of anything else to say.

Lucy turned onto the dirt road, leading to Adam's property. "You crossed the police line," I said.

"No, I didn't."

"There was a sign, saying 'Active crime scene. Do not enter.'"

"I didn't see it," she said and kept driving.

"Fair enough."

Our Thelma and Louise moment ended quickly because Margie was standing in front of Adam's house with her hands on her ample hips in her black pantsuit. I rolled down my window.

"It's not what it looks like," I said, trying to think of a lie to tell her about why we broke through a crime scene warning.

"No problem," she said. "Remington said you would probably show up." Lucy and I got out of the car. "Put on these footies and gloves, and it'll all be good. Remington's inside, doing his thing."

I wasn't used to law enforcement condoning my snooping, but I didn't give Margie another minute to change her mind. Lucy and I put on the gloves and footies and walked inside. Remington was in the kitchen, handling the forensics. He turned around and pulled his mask down off his face.

"Hey, there, sexy. How's it hangin'?"

"Hi, Remington," I said. Lucy batted her eyelids and twirled her hair. Remington looked a lot like The Rock, but he had hair, and in his CSI uniform, he was even sexier. "Do you have any clues about the murder?"

"The dude had a lot of blood in him, which bled out, and he had weird taste in pets. You can't imagine the creepy crawlers I found in this place."

"So, they're gone?" I asked looking at the floor by my feet.

"As far as I know. He had some wacky hiding places, but I think I got them all. In terms of the murder, the guy was stabbed with a kitchen knife, but not one of his knives, as far I can tell. He was dead when he was stuffed into the fridge, and the blood was mopped up with paper towels and tossed in the trash. A killer with a cleaning fetish. Go figure."

"I think the killer was trying to keep the murder a secret for as long as possible," I said.

"Could be. So, you want to do me a favor?"

"I'll do you a favor," Lucy said, twirling her hair.

"Thanks," he said. "Can you take a look at his office? There's ten tons of paper in there, and we just don't have the manpower to sift through it. Margie will work with you."

I smiled at him. I might not have been a genius, but I did recognize when I was getting special treatment. Remington knew I was there to stick my nose in, and instead of giving me a hard time, he was making an excuse so that I could do just want I wanted to do.

He winked at me, and I blushed.

Lucy and I walked into the office, and Margie came in a few seconds later. "Remington said you're a whiz bang at this kind of research," Margie told me. "Where should we start?"

"We're looking for any correspondence or notes about Jonathan Burger. And about Rachel Knight," I added on a hunch. Two deaths within a small group of friends was a big coincidence, as far as I was concerned.

Even with three people working, we barely made a dent in the papers by the time Remington finished processing the murder scene. We didn't find anything more than I found with Spencer. Lots of discussions between Adam and my father about *Fart Boy*. Nothing personal. Nothing about Rachel. There might have been more in the office, but it would have to wait until another day.

"That was boring," Lucy complained on the drive home. "I heard Bridget did hand-to-hand combat against a guy in a cardigan. All I got to do is look through papers. I didn't even get a papercut."

"I guess we could search for the Komodo dragon," I suggested. "That would be dangerous."

"Nah. I have to be home for dinner. We still have that Italian chef, and Harry wants us to get our money's worth. I've already gained three pounds. Next week, we're getting a Japanese chef. It's like those subscription services where you get a new mascara every month, except with us, it's a chef."

Boy, they say money doesn't buy happiness, but it sure buys everything else.

Dropping me off at the curb in front of my grandmother's house, Lucy said, "Let me know if you sense another murder or general mayhem and call me, so I can be there."

"Sure thing, but I doubt there'll be another murder."

"Gladie, you're a murder magnet. Sooner or later, there'll be another murder."

She was so right. "No, there won't," I said.

She rolled her eyes, honked her horn, and drove away.

I hurried inside because my grandmother hadn't eaten since this morning, and I was sure she was starving. But when I entered her bedroom, she was sitting up in bed, watching the news. Meryl was with her, and they had ordered a couple pizzas, two big bottles of Coke, salad with blue cheese dressing, and a dozen chocolate chip cookies.

"Hello, dolly," Grandma said. "Nothing, huh?"

I knew what she was asking: Did I make progress in

finding out about my father's death? "Not yet."

"I'm eating pizza for my PTSD," Meryl announced. "And I'm taking a week's leave right here with Zelda to try and recover from the Sharpie incident. I've got a cot and thirty-five romances downstairs. Can you ask Spencer to lug all that up for me?"

"Sure. I think he's hunting the dragon right now." Or the dragon was hunting him. It was a toss up.

"He just got home," Grandma said. "And he needs hydration. Bring him one of the pizzas and a bottle of Coke."

I took the food and ran downstairs, just as the door opened. "Spencer?" I asked.

"Maybe," he answered, limping into the house. "I don't know anymore."

His suit was destroyed. His pants were torn off at the knees, and his jacket only had one sleeve. His tie was turned around so that it was running down his back. His hair was standing up on end, and his face was smudged with black streaks and a green blob on his left cheek. His usually straight back was slumped.

"What happened to your shoe?" I asked. He was only wearing one.

"Who knows? It's all a blur at this point. Maybe it's in the same place as my dignity. Lord knows that'll never be found again."

CHAPTER 13

Our matches are looking for love, bubbeleh. But they're also looking for belonging. They want to be normal and to fit into the community. They want titles like, husband, wife, homeowner, parent, PTA member. That sort of thing. They want those titles. Ache for those titles. You may see an electrical bill, but to them, they see belonging. You may see a recliner chair, but to them, they see comfort, maturity, and security. Matchmaking is an iceberg, but love and attraction are only the tip. There's a lot more underneath that's just as important, and it's keeping the iceberg afloat.

Lesson 106, Matchmaking advice from your Grandma Zelda

I put the pizza down, but I handed him the Coke. "Drink this, Spencer. It'll help."

He stared out into space. "Nothing'll help. I'll still be

Police Chief Spencer Bolton, the man who let a dragon loose on a small town and got treed in front of the world's tabloids. And there's worse, Pinky. Please don't ask me about it."

I bit my lip, trying not to ask him about it. I helped him upstairs and undressed him so that he could take a shower and wash away the poisonous dragon juice and the humiliation. As I undressed him, he undressed me, too. I figured that was because of shock or Spencer being Spencer. When he stepped into the shower, he pulled me in with him.

"You're horny even now?" I asked him.

"It's my therapy, Pinky. You wouldn't want to deprive me of my therapy?"

"What kind of therapy is putting your hand between my legs?"

"It's the no-talking therapy. It's a really good therapy. I've almost forgotten about the dragon. If you turn around, I'll show you how I forget about the rest of it."

I turned around. Surprisingly, Spencer's therapy was the same as mine, although I was thinking about the pizza a little bit, too. After our shower, where, ironically, we got down and dirty, we both dressed in jeans and sweaters. Spencer brought Meryl's cot and belongings upstairs and installed her in my grandmother's bedroom.

Spencer put his wallet in his pocket and grabbed his keys. "Come on, Pinky. We're late."

"Late for what?"

"Our appointment with the sofa guy. Come on. We have to be there in ten minutes."

"What's a sofa guy?"

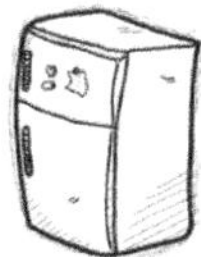

The sofa guy was a warehouse halfway to San Diego. It was run by a small group of hipsters, who all had man buns, tattoos on their knuckles and other places, and tool belts around their hips.

"Pinky, this is Perry." Spencer introduced me to the head hipster, who had brilliant blue eyes and a nose ring.

"You're going to love what we got going on here, man," he said to Spencer. "Have you ever seen Ko Phi Phi Le at sunset when the sunlight shimmers off the sand, and the water glistens like a beautiful woman who's just fallen in love with you? Well, that's what we're doing with your couch, man. And your couch too, babe."

"Thanks, dude," I said.

He walked us past a lot of other couches in different stages of being built. I didn't know what Ko Phi Phi Le was, but it probably was a lot like what was happening in the warehouse. It was every man's wet dream. Big, comfortable couches with massage settings and drink holders and whatever else was in a man's heart.

The hipster stopped us in the center of the warehouse. "I covered it to give you the drama it deserves." Spencer was riveted, his pupils dilated. He was hanging on every word and gesture of the hipster, who ripped the cover off the couch, like a Vegas magician. "Ta da, motherfucker."

Spencer clutched at his chest and sucked air. "It's everything," he breathed.

It was a couch.

It was a really big leather couch.

Spencer wrapped his arm around my waist and pulled me in close. "Our couch, Pinky. It's our couch."

"It's amazing. Really," I said.

This was marriage. Pretending to be excited about a couch.

"We still have some touches to do on it, but it'll be done and delivered the day you said," the hipster told us. Spencer hugged him hard.

"I love you, man," Spencer said.

"I love you, too, man. You want to talk about the media room chair?"

"We have a media room?" I asked and scratched my arm. Uh oh. I was getting another dose of house hives.

"We're going to have every channel in the world," Spencer gushed, smiling wide.

My phone buzzed with a text message, and I checked it.

"Roman Strand wants to see me," I told Spencer. "He has something to tell me."

"Let's go," he said, surprising me.

"Aren't you going to tell me to stay out of it?"

"Would it make a difference?"

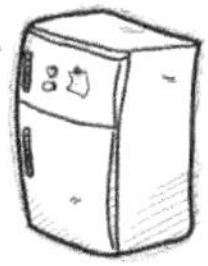

On the way to Roman's mansion, Spencer let it slip why he wanted me to talk to Roman. "He's got friends in high places, and he won't talk to us."

He meant Roman wouldn't talk to the police. "Isn't he a suspect?"

"Well, that's the thing, his alibi is his wife, and her alibi is her husband. So, I'm stuck between a rock and a dragon."

"And bubble gum. Don't forget the bubble gum," I reminded him.

"The bubble gum stuff has died down, either because the bandits ran out of bubble gum or because they've moved on."

I knew there was a "phase three" brewing, but I didn't think that Spencer needed to know that I had hired one of the bubble gum bandits and that I had gotten that tidbit of information from him.

"So you want me to interrogate Roman and get him to confess?" I asked, cracking my knuckles.

"No, I want you to get him to open the door so that I can interrogate him with my charm and style."

"I have charm and style," I said, but we both knew that wasn't true. Spencer was a metrosexual hottie with impressive muscles and a gun. I was known for finding dead people and occasionally blowing up town landmarks.

"You have charm and style for me, Pinky," Spencer said like a man who didn't want to jeopardize his sex life.

"So you think Roman did it? Do you think he killed my father and Adam Mancuso? As far as I can see, we're down to three suspects for my father's murder."

"We don't know if your father was murdered. We don't know if Adam Mancuso had enemies or if a crazy fan decided to slice and dice him. Pretty much, we don't know anything."

I thought Spencer was wrong. We knew a lot. We knew my father had a small group of friends, and he wound up dead. And we knew that we spoke about my father with those friends, and then one of them wound up dead, too.

Thinking about that reminded me about another dead friend of my father's. Rachel Knight, the depressed poet who killed herself. Something in me made me sure that her death was important to discovering the truth about my father and Adam. I didn't think that Spencer would let me dive into the files on her death, but I now had a young person at my disposal, who knew how to use a computer. I wondered how much he could find out for me.

Spencer parked in Roman's driveway. The valet was gone, but the mansion was lit up with lights in every window, as if they were having another party. I rang the doorbell, and Joy answered immediately, making me suspect that she had been watching for our arrival.

"Oh, my poor sweet Gladys," she said, inviting me in

and wrapping me in a big hug. "You've had such a hard life, and now this. Come in, my poor sweet girl."

I leaned into her, enjoying the attention and the hugging. We walked into the living room, and she sat me down next to her on the couch. There was a roaring fire in the gigantic stone fireplace, even though it was seventy-five degrees outside. Joy pointed to a platter on the coffee table with cheeses, meats, and fruit.

"May I serve you?" she asked me. "A little cheese will put the bloom back in your cheeks."

I touched my cheeks. I didn't know the bloom had left them. "I like cheese," I said.

She made me a plate with a selection of food and handed it to me. I popped a grape into my mouth. It was delicious. Rich people even had better grapes.

"Help yourself," she told Spencer, who sat in a big comfy chair. He took a slice of cheese. "Roman was so upset about Adam, but like me, he was more upset for you. How tragic that you reached out to Jonathan's friends and then this happened. You poor, sweet girl."

She touched my hand and gave it a gentle squeeze. I put my head on her shoulder and put a slice of salami in my mouth. I liked being babied.

"It was awful," I said.

"I bet. I can't even think of it. We have the security company doing double drive-bys until the craven killer is caught." There was a pregnant pause, when I figured she was giving Spencer the evil eye for not catching the craven killer.

"I hope the police find the killer, too," I said.

"I'm so glad you're in our life, again," Joy gushed, holding me close. "I can't tell you how much it means to us. Your father's passing put a big hole in our lives, especially for Roman."

"What's all this maudlin talk?" Roman asked, walking into the room. Spencer stood and shook his hand. I ate another grape.

"Not maudlin. I'm just relieved that Gladys is safe and in our lives," Joy told her husband.

"Oh, well, that's true." Roman grabbed a slice of salami and plopped down in a chair. "We were shaken up by what happened to Adam."

He said it like it happened years ago, but it was only the night before. Instead of showing real concern, it seemed to me like Roman was dismissing it like some far away event that had little or no impact on him.

"Last night, we left before Adam," Spencer said. "What did he talk to you about when we were gone?"

"Nothing," Roman said. "Nothing relevant. Adam wasn't a big talker. He drank his cognac and left."

"Any comment, any words that you can remember might give us the clues we need to find his killer," Spencer continued.

"I told you, he didn't say much," Roman grumbled and slapped his knee.

"I'm not sure I appreciate your tone, Spencer," Joy said, coming to her husband's defense.

"There's a man who was murdered, and I'm just trying to honor him by finding out why and by whom," Spencer said. I was impressed he used "whom" instead of "who."

"I have nothing further to say about Adam," Roman announced. "Gladys, there's something I wanted to talk to you about. Would you come with me?"

He stood and gestured to me. I stood, and so did Spencer.

"Just Gladys," Roman told Spencer. I grinned at my fiancé. So much for his charm.

"I'll be right back. Wait here, okay?" I gave Spencer a kiss on the cheek and whispered, "Neener, neener."

Spencer didn't look happy to let me go alone with Roman. I didn't know if he was frightened for my safety, or if he was just upset that he couldn't get a word out of Roman, but I was actually invited to talk with him.

I left Spencer with Joy, and I followed Roman through the house. We walked through hallway after hallway until he opened a side door and turned on a light. "Come on in," he said.

I walked through the doorway to find a large garage. There were three cars parked in it, and a large area, filled with organized tools and various odds and ends.

Roman turned toward me. "I loved your father," he said, softly. "He was my mentor, my brother. And you know, he was a genius. If he had lived, there would have been no stopping him. World's greatest living poet. That sort of thing."

My throat grew thick, and it was hard to swallow. I was proud of my father, but hearing about how wonderful he was just made missing him more painful.

"Now with this Adam thing, I feel that I'm coming under suspicion."

"No," I lied. "I'm sure that Spencer was just trying to find out more about Adam. He doesn't suspect you of any wrongdoing."

"Jonathan was so happy for me that night of my book release party. I signed a book for him, and he told me that he was more excited about my book than he was about his own. Can you imagine? No writer says that. It's like a mother saying she loves your child more than she loves her own. But he meant it. He wasn't a bullshitter. I'm telling you all of this so you understand how close we were. After he died, I wanted no part of the rest of his group, and sadly enough, that included your mother and you by extension. But I'm glad you're back in my life, and to prove it to you, I want to show you something."

I couldn't imagine what he wanted to show me. More than one man had told me that he wanted me in his life and wanted to show me something to prove it, and in all of those cases, I had to run out of the room. I braced myself for Roman to turn out to be a dirty, old man, intent on making a pass at me in his garage, while his wife was in the house.

But instead of lunging for me, he walked to the corner of his garage. Something was covered with a tarp. He grasped the edge of the tarp, and I was reminded of the hipster sofa guy, saying, "Ta da, motherfucker." Roman didn't say that. He yanked the tarp away, revealing a mass of twisted metal.

"I saved it all these years," Roman told me. "Your father's motorcycle."

CHAPTER 14

Don't pre-judge. Don't jump to conclusions. Don't Google. Google… What a weird name. Where does that come from? Google. Shmoogle. Phlemoogle. Weird. Why isn't it called something nice like, Jerry? Jerry is a nice name, don't you think so, dolly? Dictionaries have Webster, so, the internet should have Jerry. Anyway, don't give your matches too much information. Otherwise, they'll Google the hell out of their potential match, and it'll all go to hell. Keep them in the dark until the right moment.

Lesson 126, Matchmaking advice from your Grandma Zelda

"What?" I asked.

"Your father's motorcycle. I couldn't let them dump it, so I saved the bike. I've kept it with me all this time."

I walked forward, slowly. It barely looked like a

motorcycle, anymore. The tires were gone. The seat was gone, too. At least, I thought it was. It was a mass of twisted metal and obvious proof that my father couldn't have survived his accident.

I reached out and touched the metal. It was cool to the touch. My grandmother had hated the motorcycle, begged my father not to ride it. But it was just a bunch of metal. My father was the part that made it dangerous.

"You see, I loved him. I couldn't let him go, so I kept a piece of him," Roman said.

"Were you there at the accident? Did you see him?"

"Me? No. Not me. I heard that they were going to dump the bike after, so I picked it up."

It was a souvenir of my father, but I didn't want to see it, didn't want to be near it. Everyone grieves in their own way, but there was something about Roman keeping my father's motorcycle that bothered me. I just couldn't pinpoint what it was.

"What did Adam talk to you about after I left last night?" I asked him.

"He told me that I'm a pretentious jerk, who was a one-hit-wonder but couldn't manage a second book."

"He didn't talk about my father?" I asked.

"Adam didn't care about your father. Adam lived in his own world and didn't have room for other people. Why else would he live with a Komodo dragon and poisonous spiders?"

He had a point. "That's beside the point," I said. "He

sought my father's opinions on *Fart Boy*."

"He did?" Roman asked, honestly surprised.

"My father never helped you?"

"Of course, he did. I just didn't know that he helped Adam." Roman put his arm around my shoulders. "If you need anything from me, and I mean anything, just call. I want to be there for you. I owe it to Jonathan."

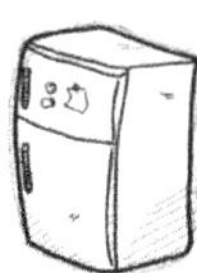

Spencer drove us away from Roman and Joy's mansion, after Roman showed me his garage. "I thought you were going to follow me into the garage and protect me," I told Spencer. "Normally, you're protective. Does this mean you don't love me anymore?"

"Well, I weighed the amount of danger you could be in against the fact that Roman's knees cracked when he walked."

"I don't get it."

"I figured you could outrun him, if it came to that. Also, Joy was an obvious admirer of the Spencer physique, so I thought I could squeeze her for information."

"How did the squeezing go?"

"She was one of those oranges that looks like it's full of juice, but is as dry as a bone when you peel it. How did it go with Roman?"

"He had the remains of my father's motorcycle

hidden away in his garage." I shivered.

"Whoa. I didn't see that one comin'."

"He said it was proof of how much he loved my father."

"I'll get my guys to pick it up in the morning," Spencer said. "Doubtful there's any forensics on it after all these years, but you never know."

"Hey, wait a minute. I thought you said my father's accident was just an accident."

Spencer ran his hand over his hair. "You don't believe it was an accident, and maybe you're contagious. Like the flu."

"You're so romantic."

"You want romance? I've got your romance right here." He was smirking his little smirk, and he had definitely moved on to a different subject. Maybe he was trying to lighten the mood and get my mind off my father's death, or maybe he was just being his usual horny self. "I'll romance the hell out of you, Pinky. Let's get home to get down to some dirty romance. Naked romance. That's the most romantic of all romance, especially when I'm naked. All kinds of huge romance. Big, huge, well-endowed naked romance."

"Okay, I get it," I said. "You're porn star material. You're King Kong."

"King Kong wishes he were me. Big, huge, romance Spencer. King Kong may be king of the jungle, but I'm king of the world. King of the bed. King of the Pinky."

"King of the Pinky?"

"King of the Pinky happy bits. Delicious, hot Pinky happy bits. Sonofabitch!"

Spencer screamed and the car swerved. The car ran up the side of the road before Spencer got control of it, again and stopped. "Did you see that?" he screamed.

"Are we talking about your shlong, again? Were you swerving out of the way of your shlong? The whole shlong bit is getting out of hand. And no, that's not a double entendre."

"Stay calm," he said and got out of the car. I got out, too, and now I could see what had made Spencer swerve. In the middle of the road was Adam's dragon. It was bigger than I had remembered.

"I think it's a dinosaur," I said.

"It's a Komodo dragon. Dinosaurs are extinct."

"I've seen *Jurassic Park*. I know what I'm looking at."

It was huge, a lot bigger than Spencer thought his manhood was. It was walking down the center of the road, like it had someplace it needed to get to.

"This is the fucker that treed me," Spencer said. "He humiliated me in front of every major tabloid. I'm a meme and a GIF, now, Pinky. Me."

"That's rough." The dragon turned its head toward Spencer and changed directions toward him. "We should probably call someone. He seems like he's out to get you."

"What do you mean, call someone?" Spencer demanded. "I'm someone. I've sworn to uphold the safety of this town."

"I think that was the line in *Jurassic Park* before the

dinosaur ate the guy."

Spencer tugged at his shirt. He looked terrified. "I'm going to do this."

"You don't sound convinced."

"I hate little lizards, Pinky. This is a little lizard times a billion. But I'm going to do this. I'm going to do this. I'm going to do this."

"You said that."

He put his hands on his hips. "Well, I am."

"Are you going to shoot it?"

"Great idea!" Then, he shook his head and looked down at his feet. "No, I can't do that. We'll have the animal rights activists after us, again, if I do that."

I had had some problems with animal rights activists when I had attacked an assistance snake. He was right. Shooting the dragon wouldn't be a good idea.

"It's coming this way," I pointed out.

"Stay clear." Spencer opened his trunk and took out a roll of duct tape. "All right. Here's what we're going to do. I'm going to capture him by his tail, and you're going to wrap the duct tape around his mouth so he can't kill us."

"I'm sensing a flaw in this plan."

"It'll work." Spencer grabbed my arm and looked into my eyes. "I'm not going to be treed again. I'm not going to be a meme, again."

The truth is that I didn't want to be anywhere near the mouth of a Komodo dragon, but it meant a lot to Spencer so that he could get his pride back, and I knew he would have done more than that for me if I asked.

I took the duct tape from him. "If it eats my arm, then maybe you could shoot it," I suggested.

"Sure thing, Pinky."

That was all of the planning we did before Spencer emitted a rebel yell and determinedly ran after the dragon with his eyes closed. Luckily, he opened them right before he reached the dragon. He circled around it, in order to get to its tail, but the dragon whipped around, almost biting Spencer.

Spencer yelled again, this time less like a little girl and more like Tarzan. He and the dragon went round and round, like wrestlers who don't touch. Finally, after several harrowing near misses, Spencer caught the dragon by the tail, clutching it with both hands.

"Holy shit! Holy shit! I got him!" Spencer screamed, this time, definitely sounding like a little girl. The dragon wasn't taking it sitting down. It tried to bite Spencer, while Spencer tried to hold on. The result was that they moved down the road in a zigzag, as if Spencer was pushing a reptile vacuum.

"Okay, Pinky, now!" Spencer shouted.

"Are you kidding me?"

"It's now or never!"

"I'm voting for never!"

"Get a good length of duct tape and go after it!"

I was probably having an aneurism, because I actually listened to him and unwrapped a long stretch of duct tape. I took a few steps toward Spencer and the dragon but then had a moment of clarity.

"This is insane," I pleaded. "Just shoot me. Shoot me instead of shooting the dragon."

"Give me a break here, Pinky." Spencer was struggling against the strength of the huge animal. His arms were wrapped around its tail, and he was working up a sweat, as he tried to hold on. The dragon didn't seem to be tiring at all, and if I could have bet money on who would have won the battle, I would have bet everything on the dragon.

But since I was in a relationship, I knew it was my responsibility to be supportive.

"You're doing a wonderful job," I told Spencer. "You are soooo strong."

"Duct tape, Pinky! Duct tape!"

I held out the piece of duct tape with both hands, like I was using it to measure curtains. The dragon was whipping around from left to right. There was no way for me to get the duct tape wrapped around its mouth without getting eaten alive.

"Pinky, duct tape!"

I leaned down and jumped back. Then, I leaned down and jumped back, again. Nope, it wasn't going to happen. I threw the piece of duct tape at the dragon and hoped for the best. The tape floated to the ground, missing the dragon entirely. Meanwhile, Spencer struggled more against the dragon, his grasp tenuous.

"Oh, come on!" Spencer yelled, frustrated with my lack of ability to duct tape a dragon's mouth.

"I can't! He'll bite me!"

"Okay. Okay. I'm going to hold its head, and then can you put the duct tape on it?" Spencer asked.

"You're going to hold the tail *and* the head?"

Spencer was out of breath when he spoke. "I'm…going…to…try…" He clutched more of the dragon's tail and moved up its body. The dragon didn't like this at all. Spencer did a dance to avoid the dragon's mouth, and then in one swift movement, Spencer put his foot on top of the dragon's head, immobilizing it.

"You did it!" I yelled. "You really are strong. Before, I was just saying it to be nice, but you really are strong."

"Duct tape!"

"Right. Here I go."

I tried to unroll the tape, but I couldn't get it unstuck. I should have folded over a little piece when I had ripped off a section, but I hadn't thought of it, and now it was stuck onto the roll, and there was no way to peel it off.

"Duct tape!" Spencer shouted. The dragon was putting up a valiant fight. Spencer was clutching its tail to his chest and had one foot on the dragon's mouth. There wasn't a doubt in my mind that this wasn't going to end well, but I knew I would still love Spencer as much if he only had one foot.

And he probably was only going to have one foot by the time this was over.

And it was probably going to be over soon.

"I don't have long fingernails," I explained. "I can't

get the tape."

"Pinky, I'm not sure I can love you if you don't get the duct tape around this beast's mouth before it bites my foot off."

I worked feverishly at the roll of duct tape. Finally, I managed to unroll a long piece. "I did it! I did it! Here I come." Hovering over the dragon, I looked up at Spencer. "You got it, right? You're not going to let it bite me, right?"

"Duct tape!"

I stuck the tape on its mouth and ripped off another section. In a blur, Spencer let go of the tail, grabbed the tape and wrapped a second layer around the dragon's mouth, this time tighter. Five more layers, and we were reasonably sure it was safe to be around the dragon.

Spencer hugged me tight. "That was the grossest thing I've ever done, and I belonged to a fraternity in college," he said.

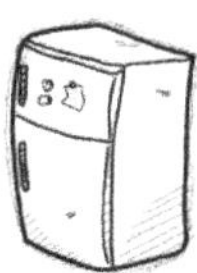

We drove to the Historic District with the Komodo dragon in the trunk of Spencer's car. We stopped at a corner where there was a big crowd, so that Spencer could show off the captured dragon. By the time he was finished describing his valiant triumph over the monster, he was surrounded by America's tabloids, the entire DICK contingent, half of the town, and three animal control teams, to whom Spencer handed the dragon over. They had all come around with the news that Spencer had a dragon in his car.

"The dragon wasn't hurt during its capture," Spencer announced to the crowd. Originally, he wanted to give me half the credit for snagging the dragon, but I decided it was better to lay low and not get any more attention than I needed from the tabloids and a lot of DICK.

Afterward, Spencer and I split up, each going our own way. I walked to my grandmother's, while Spencer drove to the police station, where he was going to continue being the town's big hero. It was a beautiful evening, and I felt lucky to live in a place where I could walk alone in the evening without fear. There was little or no crime in Cannes. That is, except for the murders that seemed to happen just about every month since I had moved in with my grandmother nearly a year before.

Thinking about murder reminded me of something that Joy had told me that got the hair on the back of my neck standing up. I sped up and arrived home a few minutes later. I checked on Grandma and Meryl, quickly. Grandma was taking a nap and snoring, while Meryl was reading a Melissa Foster romance.

I climbed up to the attic and turned on my laptop. Googling Roman's book, I discovered that it had been published less than a week before my father died. "Holy shit," I said.

I grabbed my phone and made the call to my mother's prison farm. It was a complicated process to get through to her, but finally she was on the phone. "Hi, Gladie," she said, sweetly. I looked at my phone. It was still disorienting having my mother be nice. I guessed farming really was therapeutic.

"Hi. I have a question," I said finally. "Do you remember Roman Strand's book release party?"

"I wore an off-the-shoulder dress," she answered, remembering. "It was a very fancy party. Roman took to being successful like a duck to water. One minute he was a nobody like the rest of us, and the next minute, he was Mister Fancypants. He loved it."

"What did Dad think about Roman's success?"

"He was thrilled for him. No jealousy. He even made a toast to him. Then, Roman signed one of his books to him, like he was gifting your father with a block of gold. I don't remember what happened after that."

"Nothing," I said. "Dad was dead within a week."

"He was? How could I have forgotten that timeline?"

I didn't know, and neither did she, and we had run out of things to say to each other. A minute later, we said goodbye and hung up.

I looked around the attic, as if the answers I was looking for could be found in the dusty corners. My eyes landed on my father's box, and I picked it up and put it on the folding table. I had never finished going through it. Perhaps there were more clues.

Before I could start searching the box, my phone rang. "Gladys Burger?" a voice asked.

"Yes. Who is this?"

"Steve Byrne, the insurance broker. I need to talk to you."

My skin erupted in goosebumps. "You do?"

"Come to my house. Don't tell anyone. It's important. I'm coming, Poopykins. Daddy loves you. Daddy loves you. Yes, I do. Yes, I do." His voice trailed off in sickeningly sweet baby talk, and it was obvious that he was talking to his hyper-spoiled dog.

"Why do you want me to come to your house?" I asked, trying to get his attention. "I don't need insurance."

"Everyone needs insurance," he insisted. "You never know what will happen to you in this life. Death might be right around the corner. A heartbeat away. Or you could fall down the stairs or get hit by a bus. It happens every day. Every minute of every day, even."

"I don't need insurance," I repeated, but I sounded less sure.

"Fine. But watch out for buses. And come over. I won't try to sell you insurance."

I struggled between worrying if it was safe to trust him and wanting to squeeze him for information. "Why do you want me to come over?"

"Isn't it obvious?" he asked. "I know who murdered Adam. And your father, for that matter."

CHAPTER 15

Matchmaking is an art and a business, dolly. You have the gift for the art, but it might take some learning to figure out the business part. I decided not to learn the business part at all, and it's worked for me, but every once in a while, I wonder if I should have an index fund or buy bonds. Then, it goes away, and I'm back to thinking about love. But you should think a little about the business part. Take care of the books and prepare for rainy days. Rainy days never seem to come in batches of only one. When there's one, there's usually one right after, and maybe another after that.

Lesson 124, Matchmaking advice from your Grandma Zelda

I called Lucy. "What are you doing? Are you busy?" I asked her.

"The chef made us a delicious dinner, Gladie. You

should have come over. I'm about ready to explode. I couldn't move if I wanted to. I took off my pantyhose, and I'm about to lie in bed and read a magazine. I might never move again, Gladie. Carbs are the devil. That's a bit of wisdom from this woman to you. Carb coma, that's what I've got goin' on now, darlin'. What about you? What are you up to? Are you doing something with Spencer?"

"No, he's busy being a hero and letting the town tell him how wonderful he is."

"He is? What kind of wonderful? What did he do?"

"He captured the dragon," I told her. "I helped him, but don't tell anyone. I don't want to relive that experience."

"You helped Spencer capture a dragon? You did that while I was eating pasta?"

"I haven't showered since then. I have dragon slobber goo all over me. I'm going to have to burn my clothes."

Lucy harrumphed. "I miss everything. My life is boring, Gladie. Nothing happens in my life."

"You have a chef. You're married."

"What's your point?"

What was my point? Did I have a point? "Everyone wants boring, Lucy. Boring comes with a washer and dryer." There was a long silence on the phone. "Lucy? You there?"

"I was just trying to figure out if we're talking about me or you, and if I should ask how you and Spencer are doing."

It was a good time to change the subject. "Anywho, I called because something might be happening, and I wanted to know if you'd like to go with me."

"Yes."

"But the carb coma."

"I don't care about the carb coma. What's going to happen? Another dragon? A dead body? Gladie, was there another murder?" She was buzzing with energy. I told her about the call from Steve. "Oh! A confession. That's pretty good but not really exciting."

"Well, I have a feeling..."

"Well, what? Gladie, do you have a funny feeling, like Zelda gets? Oh, I knew it. I knew it. You have the magical murder mojo. Should I bring my Taser?"

"Probably. And do you have any leftover pasta?"

It wasn't until after I picked up Lucy, that I realized I didn't know where Steve lived. I called him, but it went to voicemail. "Steve Byrne. Happy to make your life more secure. I can't come to the phone right now, but even if I've met with some horrible accident, I'm not worried because I'm covered. Leave a message after the beep and leave me your contact information so that I can cover you, too." It beeped, and I left a message, asking for his address.

"I got this, darlin'," Lucy told me when I hung up. She thumbed a bunch of buttons on her phone and came up with an address. "Look at that. Mr. Insurance Man lives near

Bridget."

It was dark out, and Cannes was quiet. The townspeople were acting normal for once, staying inside, watching TV and eating snack food. Lucy was staring out the window, her body like a panther, ready to strike.

"We're just going to talk to him," I told her.

"I know. I've got my Taser."

"He sells insurance."

We got out of the car and walked up the walkway to his townhouse. "What are you carrying?" I asked Lucy.

"My shovel. I forgot that I had left it in your backseat."

"I don't think we need a shovel."

"It's six feet long. I could bean him over the head and not get anywhere near him."

"Okay. Bring it. But be nonchalant with it."

"I'll pretend I'm going gardening after," Lucy said. She was wearing a chiffon dress, cinched at the waist with a wide belt and then flared out to her knees with strappy high heels.

"Okay. Tell him you're gardening."

Lucy rang the doorbell, and I knocked on the door. When I knocked, the door swung open with a soft creaking noise. Lucy and I looked at each other. "This is how it happened the last time," I whispered to her.

Lucy lifted up her shovel, like she was cleanup batter at the World Series.

"Steve, it's Gladie. You called me to come over," I

announced. "Steve?"

There was no answer. Lucy and I looked at each other. "If we were smart, we would call Spencer," I whispered to her.

Lucy stomped her delicate shoe on the ground. "Don't steal my fun, Gladie," she said, but there was a distinct tone of wariness in her voice.

I stuck my head in the house. Every light was on, but there was no sign that anyone was home. "Steve? Steve, it's Gladie. You told me to come here."

Finally, there was a sound. And it was coming toward us. *Click. Click. Click.* And there was the sound of a little bell, too. Lucy choked up on her shovel, wielding it like Hank Aaron.

"We're just talking with him," I whispered, reminding her.

"Okay, but I want to be ready to smack him to lights out."

It sounded wise to me. I liked having backup. "Just a second. Let's calm down a little. This is Steve, the insurance salesman. We have nothing to fear from an insurance salesman."

But was that true? He was my most obvious suspect. He had means, motive, and opportunity. He was jealous of his friends' success. Instead of famous with a mansion and a dragon, he was hawking home, fire, and life and lived in a townhouse. That spelled murder to me.

The clicking and bell ringing got closer. Lucy was

poised to strike with her shovel, and I was poised to run like hell. Then, we saw the source of the noise.

It was Poopykins.

Lady Philomena.

Steve's dog.

Lucy and I erupted in laughter, giggling like schoolgirls and hugging each other while we tried to catch our breath. "Just a dog. Just a dog," I breathed. "We're being so silly."

The dog clicked away, deeper into the townhouse, and I took two steps inside. "Steve, it's Gladie! Are you decent?"

I gestured for Lucy to follow me. The townhouse looked a lot like Steve. It had generic, cheap furniture, no artwork, several piles of mail on a table next to the front door, and a lot of dog paraphernalia. No sign of Steve, himself. The townhouse was set up like Bridget's with three small levels.

"Maybe he's hiding, waiting to kill you," Lucy suggested in a whisper.

"What about you? Isn't he waiting to kill you, too?"

"Nobody tries to kill me. They're always after you. But I've got your back. I'll whack him with my shovel and then fry his testicles."

"Okay." It was a good plan, except for the possibility of me being already dead when she fried his testicles. "Normal people would call the police," I said.

"Normal people… funny one, Gladie."

The main floor was a living room with the regular

living stuff. I searched it for signs that Steve was the murderer, or if he was telling me the truth and knew who the killer was, any clues about who that was. I found a bunch of different insurance brochures and a disturbing amount of dog photos, but there was nothing about my father or Adam.

"We're going to have to go to the other floors," I whispered to Lucy.

"Downstairs or upstairs?" she whispered back. Her head darted from left to right, watching for Steve with her shovel raised. The townhouse hugged the side of a canyon. The main floor was the middle floor. The dog's bell on its collar dinged as it went downstairs.

"I guess we follow the dog," I said. "Keep your shovel ready."

Even though Lucy was the one who was armed, she walked closely behind me. She had my back, but nobody had my front. Before we reached the stairs, I grabbed a dog bone from the floor and wielded it for my own defense. We walked slowly down the stairs. Each step creaked, announcing our descent, so if Steve was lying in wait for us, he knew we were coming. The dog's clicking had stopped, but the bell was still ringing. When I got downstairs, it became clear why. The floor was carpeted, which muffled the dog's nails when it walked. There were two bedrooms downstairs. One was used as a makeshift office, and the other was Steve's bedroom. He hadn't made his bed, and he had left wet towels on the bathroom floor. The dog circled my feet and went back upstairs. There was no sign of Steve, and I began to relax.

"Can you believe he left us alone to snoop?" I asked Lucy.

I went through Steve's desk, but all I could find were bills and insurance stuff. Nothing about my father or Adam. There wasn't any poetry, either. I supposed that when Steve quit writing, he really quit writing.

It was time to go to the top floor, the last place to search. That turned out to be the dining room and kitchen combo, just like in Bridget's townhouse. We stood in the dining area. The dog click-clicked all over the floor, circling me. This time, he left little paw prints where he stepped.

And the paw prints were red.

"Uh," I said.

"He's not up here, either," Lucy said. "What a dud. I should have stayed home and digested my Italian dinner. Nothing ever happens when I'm around. I'm a jinx."

"Uh…"

"I guess we should go. This is so disappointing. My boring life is contagious."

"Lucy, look down."

She looked down. "Cute floor design. Steve's painted the whole floor in little red paw prints."

I put my hand on her back. "Lucy, I'm going to tell you something, and you should try to remain calm."

"Is it about Spencer?" she asked, alarmed. "Is that two-timing, low down dirty dog cheating on you? I'll kill him. Worse, I'll get Harry to kill him."

I took a step back. "No, he's not cheating on me.

Why? What have you heard? Do you know something that I don't?" I wagged my finger at her. "Lucy, I swear that if you hide anything about Spencer from me, I'll kill you. I'll kill you with this bone!" I raised the dog bone over my head.

"No, darlin'. I don't know a thing. I swear it. You said you have something to tell me and to remain calm, so I assumed the worst."

"Why did you assume that?" I was panicking real bad. Images of Spencer having sex with women with no cellulite ran through my mind, and it was freaking me out. "Should I assume that? Is that something I should assume?"

"No! But why are you so worried? If there was nothing to worry about, you wouldn't be worried."

I put my hands on my hips. "Lucy, since when have I needed a reason to worry?"

"That's true. Boy, we really went down a rabbit hole. So, what did you want to tell me?"

"Thank you. I did not want to tell you anything about Spencer. Spencer and I are perfectly fine. More than fine. Smooth sailing. Lots of sex. He tells me he loves me all the time. So, there's nothing to assume where we're concerned." I took a deep breath and tried to get rid of the images of Spencer cheating from my brain. "The reason I wanted to talk to you was to tell you that the dog paw pattern on the floor is not a painted design. Look at the dog, walking around."

Lucy's mouth dropped open, and she looked down at the dog, which took a few steps, leaving faded red paw prints on the floor. "Well, shut my mouth. What is that?"

"Stay calm."

"Why do I need to stay calm? Oh," she said after a pause. "Because it's blood. Bloody paw prints all over the floor. Oh."

She swayed on her feet, and I clutched onto her. "Whoa there, girl. Are you okay?"

"Of course I am," she said, affronted. "Do you think the blood is real?"

"Yes."

"Whose blood is it?"

It was either Steve's blood or whoever was Steve's latest victim. "I don't know."

"Maybe Steve cut himself shaving," Lucy suggested. "Do you think he cut himself shaving? Maybe he's a competitive swimmer and has to shave his legs."

Lucy was in denial and making a deal with the universe that there was a simple excuse for the bloody paw prints. I recognized the symptoms of denial because I had been there before. "I think it's more than a nicked leg. I think someone's dead."

"Where's the body? There's no sign of the body." Lucy spun around, looking nervously for a body.

I had a bad feeling about where the body was. A half-wall separated the kitchen from the dining area, and we hadn't investigated the kitchen area, yet. I looked over at the refrigerator. It was the freezer on the top kind, not as big as Adam's French door fridge.

I sighed.

"I guess we should get this over with," I said. "Time to open the refrigerator."

We walked into the kitchen area behind the little wall. "You're right. His legs are cut," I said. Most of Steve was stuffed into the refrigerator, which was partially open and secured with a kitchen towel. Since the refrigerator was too small for such a big man, Steve's legs were sticking out, and they were cut and bloody.

That wasn't the only thing that was bloody. Instead of cleaning up the blood with paper towels like the killer had done with Adam, this time the killer had decided to be messy, or he just didn't have the time to be tidy, because Steve had bled out onto the kitchen's tile floor. So, there was a big pool of blood over much of the kitchen floor, which the dog had walked in.

"That's Steve, all right," I said. "I recognize his pants cuffs."

Lucy nodded. She was staring at Steve's legs, too. It was hard not to. The way they were sticking out made them look like some kind of gag gift. I half-expected Steve to jump out of a closet somewhere, laugh hysterically, and shout, "April Fools!" even though it was June, and it was obvious that Steve was deader than a doornail.

"This is a lot like what happened to Adam," I told Lucy. "Except messier. And no dragon. Just a little dog. So, you got your dose of excitement, Lucy. You happy?"

She nodded and kept staring at Steve's legs.

"Funny how just a few months ago, I would be throwing up all over the place, seeing this," I told her. "But I guess it's like eating avocados. When you try one for the first time, it tastes like snail guts on your tongue, but after you eat a few avocados, you can't get enough. It's all about the avocado on toast and avocado in salad. There's guacamole. There's avocado crema. Avocado everything. Geez, now I want an avocado. Are you hungry? Boy, I could really eat. I wonder if the grocery store is still open and if they have any ripe avocados. That's the problem with avocados. You have to get them ripe, or you're forced to put them out on the counter for days while they ripen, looking at the avocados all the time, wanting to eat them. Oh, yes, I sure am hungry. Do you like avocados? Lucy? Lucy? Did you hear me? Are you okay?"

"Blood," she said.

"Oh, yeah. Tons of it. The refrigerator must be tilted for it to have poured out like that. You could do laps in that pool of blood on the floor."

"Blood."

"Yep."

"Blood. Oh, blood. Legs. Blood. Legs. Blood. Refrigerator."

I had seen this before. Lucy was on a loop, caused by seeing lots of grossness and violence. There wasn't really a cure for it. It was sort of like colitis; you just lived with it. "Take a deep breath, Lucy. You want a glass of water? Maybe we should just get you out of here."

She made a little noise, like a mouse. Her shovel slipped out of her hand and fell onto the floor with a loud clanking noise, landing in the pool of blood, splashing and sending some blood up into the air before it splashed back down onto the floor, again.

"Oh God," Lucy moaned and fell, stiff as a board into the blood. I stared in disbelief at my friend in her beautiful dress with her once perfectly styled hair and her once perfectly made up face. Not any longer. Now, she was half submerged in Steve's blood.

"Lucy? Are you all right? Wake up," I said. It turned out that excitement didn't agree with her, after all. "Wake up. Lucy? Are you okay?"

She moaned and touched her forehead with her hand, leaving a trail of even more blood on herself. "What happened?" she asked.

"You passed out into a puddle of a murdered man's blood, and now you're completely covered in it."

"I what?"

"It could be worse," I said. "I mean, it can't be any worse. Doesn't that make you feel better? If it can't be any worse, then, you have nothing to worry about."

I heard the sound of the dog's bell, as it walked into the kitchen, sniffed Lucy's leg and began to hump it for everything she was worth. Lady Philomena humped away, going at Lucy in a reverse cowgirl position. I had never seen a female dog hump a leg, but I tried not to judge.

"What's happening?" Lucy moaned. "Why is this

happening?"

CHAPTER 16

My grandmother never ate a vegetable in her life. She survived on chicken fat, pastries sweetened with honey, and Bloody Marys for breakfast on the weekends. That woman lived until she was one-hundred-two, and she was as sharp as a tack until the day she died. My Uncle Manny played tennis for two hours a day, every day, and was a strict vegan. His annual birthday cake was a lentil loaf. That man dropped dead of a massive heart attack on the tennis court when he was fifty-two. What's my point? There's no rhyme or reason, bubbeleh. Sometimes, we think a lentil loaf is the way to go, but really, it's all about the chicken fat and Bloody Marys. A nosh for some is a meal for others. Logic has a way of being totally illogical. So does love. You think this one will love that one, but really, he'll love a totally different someone. Be open. Be flexible. Drink a Bloody Mary and relax.

Lesson 125, Matchmaking advice from your

Grandma Zelda

I wasn't hungry, anymore. The thought of avocados made me sick to my stomach. The reality of what had happened to Steve and all of the gore in front of me had hit me late, but hard. I helped Lucy out of the blood and wiped her down with a kitchen towel. Steve didn't have any paper towel, and I didn't know if that was the reason the killer didn't clean up, or if he didn't have time.

In any case, Lucy was a mess. The kitchen towel only served to smear the blood around on her skin, hair, and clothes. By the time I was done helping her, she looked like the climactic scene from *Carrie.* "This isn't exciting," Lucy said. "This is gross."

"That's kind of how it goes. There's always a certain amount of gross that goes with the excitement."

I now had Steve's blood and gore all over me, too, on top of the dragon goo slobber that was all over me. My Walley's brand jeans were ruined. Ditto my Keds. I would have to match someone, quickly so that I could afford a new outfit. If I kept finding dead bodies and dragons, I would wind up naked.

Lucy's losses were worse. Her designer outfit was worth more than my car. And where I had lost my appetite, she was green underneath the layer of blood on her face.

We stood in the kitchen, waiting for the police to arrive. Instead of calling Spencer, I made a call to the general police line, hoping that Remington would show up. He was a lot less judgmental than Spencer, and I didn't want to interrupt Spencer's hero moment to remind him that the woman he loved had a habit of disturbing crime scenes.

My call worked. Remington showed up with Margie after about five minutes. It was just in time because Lucy was pretty freaked out, and I wondered if she might need medical care. She was standing with her arms outstretched, like she was a tightrope walker.

"Look at that," Margie said and whistled long and slow. "The boss's girl did it again. How ya doin', Gladie? What's new?"

"I'm pretty sure that it's Steve Byrne in the refrigerator. He sells insurance."

"Sounds about right," Remington said and eyed Lucy. "Did you find him this way, or was it more of a progressive turn of events?"

"We found him this way, and then it was a progressive turn of events," I explained.

"Did he go after you with a shovel, and then things got out of hand?" Margie asked. She was asking if we had murdered Steve, but she was asking it in a nice way. I liked her. If I knew how to needlepoint, I would have joined her club.

"I brought the shovel," Lucy said, coming to life for a brief moment.

"You brought the shovel?" Margie asked.

Remington caught my eye and smiled, wide. "You're a G, Gladie."

I didn't know what that meant, but I figured it was a compliment. I shrugged. I told them about Steve's phone call and finding him. "And we didn't actually use the shovel."

"Makes sense," Remington said, nodding.

"It sort of makes sense," Margie said. "In a weird, nonsense way. Did you find any strange, poisonous animals in the house?"

"No, just Lady Philomena." The dog click-clicked around us, and her bell rang.

"Poor little orphan doggie," Margie said. She picked the dog up and petted her. Lady Philomena took to Margie right away and licked her face. "Maybe I'll be her foster mama, if nobody else wants her," she suggested.

"I guess we should clear the scene," Remington said.

"Poor little doggie had a bad day," Margie said in baby talk to the dog. She held her close and sat down on the couch, petting the dog and ignoring Remington's order to clear the scene.

"I think I'd like to go home," Lucy said, finally coming back to herself. "I don't like having blood all over me."

Remington took his phone out of his pocket. "I'll let you go in a minute. First, I need to take a series of photos."

By the time he took the third photo, Spencer had arrived and marched upstairs. His eyes bugged out of his head when he saw bloody Lucy.

"It's not Lucy's blood," I told Spencer. "It's Steve's."

"Are you kidding me?"

"It's not my fault," I said. "Lucy brought the shovel."

"I cannot tell a lie. She's right. It's my shovel, darlin'," she confessed.

"Shovel?" Spencer asked. "Are you kidding me?"

"Purely for defense purposes," I explained.

Spencer put his hands over his eyes and took a deep breath. "I was having a pretty good day. The dragon was shipped to the San Diego Zoo. The tabloids are leaving town."

I put my hands on my hips. "I don't think I like your tone. You're acting like I'm to blame for this."

Spencer took a couple steps toward the kitchen. That's when he noticed Steve's legs sticking out of the refrigerator. He sucked air and said a bad word. "Why are Gladie and Lucy standing in the crime scene?" Spencer asked Remington.

"That's how I found them," Remington answered.

"Lucy, why are you in the crime scene?" Spencer asked her.

She looked at me. It was the first time she had been chastised by Spencer. Normally, I was the center of that kind of attention. And normally, I was the one to pass out in a puddle of blood, or at least the equivalent kind of mishap.

"It's not my fault," she said, tidying her hair, which was sticky with blood. "I think I'll go home now."

She was Scarlett O'Hara, a class act, Southern belle, who always remained calm, cool, and collected. Covered in blood and half in shock, she stood up straight with total dignity. A regal queen. It was amazing that she was my friend. She was foie gras, and I was corned beef hash. She was a Mercedes Benz SL, and I was an Oldsmobile Cutlass Supreme. She was the one-percent, and I was percent-less.

"Gladie, I trust that you'll drive me home."

"Of course I will," I said, sneering at Spencer.

"Spencer Bolton, I can assure you that I haven't messed up your crime scene," Lucy said. "I've been completely professional. I didn't touch a hair on the dead insurance salesman. Neither did Gladie. She was perfectly behaved from start to finish. She was just like CSI Miami. So, if you don't mind, I'll just take my shovel and get out of here."

I was touched that she had come to my defense, and I felt bad that she had been traumatized and humiliated. "I'll get it for you, Lucy," I told her. "And then I'll take you home. She's right, Spencer. We didn't touch the body. We kept your crime scene completely clean, except for the blood on the floor. Without us, you wouldn't have known that Steve was murdered. You should thank us."

I leaned over to get her shovel, but it was stuck in the sticky blood, and when I tried to pick it up, I slipped on the slick floor. I swung my arms like propellers, trying to catch my balance, but I knew I was going down.

Damn it. Served me right, trying to help.

Spencer and Remington bolted forward to try and catch me, but my fall happened too fast. Right before I was going to hit the tile floor, I grabbed the kitchen towel that had been used by the killer to partially close the refrigerator door. The move slowed down my fall, so instead of hitting the tile with a thump, I hit it relatively softly, landing on my back, lying in the pool of blood, just like Lucy a few moments before. Unfortunately, I took the kitchen towel with me when I fell. Without the towel, the refrigerator door opened, and poor, murdered Steve fell out of the fridge and landed on top of me.

It wasn't the first time I had had dead person on me, but this was the most intimate. I had the world's biggest case of cooties. Steve smelled like dead person and a ham sandwich. The sandwich must have been in the refrigerator next to his body, I thought. "Help," I said, my voice muffled. "Help. Dead. Help."

Spencer and Remington lifted the body off of me. "You contaminated the scene," Spencer insisted.

"I have dead person in my mouth," I complained. "I have dead person in my hair."

"Pinky, you make police work a bitch."

The sad thing was that it wasn't even close to the first time that I had a dead person on me.

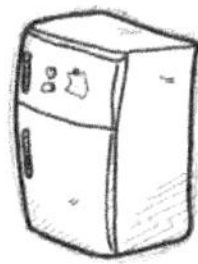

Lucy insisted that we get tetanus shots. I didn't argue.

The paramedics gave us the shots, wrapped us in blankets and afterward on Lucy's orders, Margie drove us to

Lucy's favorite spa, which was just outside of Cannes, next to the apple orchards. Lucy called ahead and ordered the Emergency Deluxe Everything package.

"We're going to erase this day, Gladie," Lucy told me in the backseat of Margie's police car.

"That sounds good."

"We'll spend the night, and by the time we wake up tomorrow morning, we'll have dewy, taut skin, and no sign of corpse."

"Or dragon?"

"Or dragon," Lucy assured me. Money sure came in handy.

I called my grandmother to check up on her and let her know that I wouldn't be back until the morning. She told me that she was fine and that she had already called Spencer to ask him to bring home sub sandwiches and barbecue chips when he returned. I felt guilty that she was still in bed because I hadn't given her closure about my father and his possible killer. In fact, I was no closer to solving the mystery. Instead, I was just accumulating more mysteries.

But if I was right at all about my father's friends being the suspects, I was now down to two. I didn't know why they would have killed my father, Adam, and Steve. It didn't make sense.

"Roman and Joy have everything," I said in the car. "Why would they take a knife and kill their friends?"

"Rich people are weird," Margie said, as she drove. "No offense, Ms. Smythe."

"No offense taken," Lucy said. "I became rich. I didn't start that way."

As far as I knew, Roman and Joy became rich, too. None of my father's friends had any money when he was alive. They had been happy in their poverty, content to center their lives around their creativity and art. It was very romantic, and it seemed that my father was the linchpin that kept it all together. When he was gone, it fell apart.

Or did it begin to fall apart when Rachel Knight killed herself the year before?

I couldn't shake the feeling that Rachel's suicide was key to this whole mystery. I also couldn't shake the feeling that if everyone connected to my father was dying, there was a chance that I could be next.

I also couldn't shake the feeling that I shouldn't tell Spencer about my feeling. He would lock me up, if he thought I was in danger.

"Look at what Spot is doing. She's the sweetest dog!" Margie exclaimed, laughing. She had quickly adopted Lady Philomena and changed her name. The dog was thrilled to ride in the front seat, next to her new mom with the window open.

"She wasn't so sweet when she was humping my leg, while she walked around in her master's blood," Lucy muttered out of the side of her mouth.

She had a point.

"Look at that," Margie said, pointing outside. "That car just went through the red light in front of this police car."

"Are you going to give him a ticket?" Lucy asked.

"Nope. That's the area's only red-light camera. He'll get his justice, all right. He'll get a big, fat ticket in the mail."

The light turned green, and we drove through the intersection, passing the other car. I recognized the driver. It was the guy who had come to my grandmother's house and picked up Draco's license plates. I turned around and watched him pull to the side and put another license plate on his car.

It was Phase Three of the resistance against DICK. I had a suspicion of whose license plates he was putting on his car before he ran the red light again. I was impressed with the cleverness of Draco's generation.

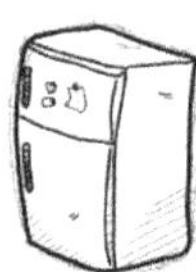

Lucy was half-right about the spa erasing the day. I was treated like Dorothy in the Emerald City. I was buffed and polished. In the end, I did have dewy skin and soft, silky hair, just like Lucy had promised. They dressed me in a cashmere track suit, and Lucy and I ate a heavenly meal. But even though the bed they provided was two feet thick with some miracle material that ensured a good night's sleep, I didn't sleep a wink.

All night, I went round and round in my mind, trying to put the puzzle pieces of the murders together. But I was missing crucial pieces of the puzzle and couldn't put it together. Early the next morning, Lucy hired a limo to take me home. I was anxious to check on my grandmother and to grill Spencer on his investigation into Steve's murder.

There were a bunch of cars and three television news vans parked in front of Grandma's house. I ran inside, worried that something had happened to my grandmother, but inside, it was all smiles. The mayor was there with his arm around Spencer, smiling for the cameras.

"Hey there, Gladie." Meryl greeted me, standing at my right, taking in the action. "It's been a madhouse here."

"How's Grandma?"

"Sleeping. She said she's going to be in bed for a while longer."

"Did she give a hint about how much longer?"

"No. She's not saying much. I read through most of my books, so I thought I'd give my eyes a rest and come down here. You're just in time. Your love bunny is getting a medal."

"A medal?"

"For the dragon thing. I should get a medal for saving the First Amendment. People's priorities are all turned around. Have you noticed?"

"Quiet, please, newspeople and people of note," the mayor announced. The reporters got into position around the mayor and Spencer. Big lights had been turned on. Spencer looked like a movie star but slightly nervous and sheepish about the attention. The mayor looked dapper, as usual, but he still sounded like an idiot.

"I've gathered you all here today to witness the medal-pinning ceremony. This is the first medal the mayor of Cannes has awarded since Frankie the Bull saved a little girl from the Mighty Frighty Gang in 1899. I have to tell you that it wasn't easy to find where the mayor hid his collection of medals from over one hundred years ago. My secretary was looking everywhere. Under the desk…nope. Secret panels in the walls…nope. Behind the toilet…nope. She didn't find the medals, but she did a spring cleaning like nobody's business. You could eat off the bathroom floor now. Believe you me. I'm not just saying that. Anybody want to come back with me after this, and we'll eat off the bathroom floor together? I could go for a brisket sandwich. Yum."

He held up a bronze medal with a green ribbon. "Old man O'Malley gave us his Bronze Star from his participation in the Battle of the Bulge in World War II. I hear that was a real doozy of a battle. Lots of tanks. O'Malley told me that Patton could fart the National Anthem. You can quote me on that. Anyway, we added the green ribbon because we thought it looked reptilian."

The mayor turned toward Spencer. "Chief Bolton, this medal is awarded to you for your valor in the face of a Komodo dragon, which was let loose on our beloved town, threatening its very survival." He gave me a pointed look, as if I was to blame for letting the dragon loose. "With little thought to your own safety, you captured the dragon and without hurting it, delivered it to the San Diego Zoo, which I hear has wonderful, humane exhibits and also sells very tasty churros. Spencer Bolton, the city of Cannes thanks you for making our beloved town a safer place, you know, except for the ten-thousand-fold increase in murders since you moved into town." He looked at me again. Then, he pinned the medal onto Spencer's chest and kissed him on both cheeks, French-style, much to Spencer's chagrin.

The reporters asked Spencer some questions, and he was good at side-stepping the actual details of the dragon's capture so that he wouldn't bring me into the mess while not taking sole credit.

Remington appeared at my left. "Hey, Gladie. How are you feeling? You okay after the fridge thing?"

"Whoa, Nelly," Meryl said, taking a gander at Remington. "Do you work out?"

"Yes, ma'am. I still train in MMA. I have a fight next week, if you're interested."

"I'd love that!" Meryl announced, perking up. "Will you be half naked?"

"And barefoot."

"That sounds invigorating."

Remington winked at me. "How about you? Are you invigorated?"

Everything about Remington was invigorating. I was tempted to reach out and touch his muscles, but the truth was that Remington was instant pudding and Spencer was a steak dinner.

"What did you find out about Steve? Was he killed like Adam?" I asked him.

"Stabbed, but this time with a smaller knife. Not his. We've been running down his schedule, leading up to his murder. We discovered that he had a side gig in insurance fraud. There might be a few people who wanted him dead. He did a lot of double-dealing, as far as we can tell."

Steve might have been into some bad stuff, but that wouldn't explain why he was killed in exactly the same way as Adam. It was obvious that they were killed by the same person.

The newspeople and onlookers applauded and filed out of Grandma's house.

Spencer shot a look at Remington and then at me. "That's my cue," Remington told me and left, too.

"Congratulations," I told Spencer.

"I have a used Bronze Star. I'm going to be on three entertainment shows for my part in capturing a reptile. This is not my finest moment, Pinky." He smelled my hair. "You smell good. Not a hint of decomp anywhere on you."

"They let me keep the track suit. It's cashmere."

"I like it. I can tell you're not wearing a bra." He leaned in and grazed a knuckle over my breast.

"Is this how you make yourself feel better?" I asked. "I use chocolate to make me feel better. Is there any chocolate?"

"C'mon, Pinky. Give a guy a break. I had to sleep alone last night."

"You can't go one night without sex?"

"No. Well, what's your definition of sex? I need at least a hand job. How about it, Pinky?"

"I'd rather eat a Hershey bar."

Spencer looked up at the ceiling. "I've got to remember to carry Hershey bars with me. I would get so much more action."

The truth was that sex with Spencer was better than a Hershey bar, but I was preoccupied. The murders were getting closer to me, and I had a feeling of dread. And fear.

"Remington said that Steve was stabbed to death, just like Adam."

"But with another knife. Not his. Are you okay, Pinky? You don't look so good. Did Remington bother you?"

"No, of course not. Why would he?"

Spencer smirked. "He wouldn't."

"He wouldn't? What did you do to him?"

He put his hands up. "I'm a gentleman, Gladie. I didn't lay hands on him. I might have told him that I would disembowel him if he ever got near you again, but I didn't lay hands on him."

"You threatened him?"

Spencer put his thumb and forefinger an inch apart. "Maybe a smidge." He smirked his normal smirk.

"You seem very happy today, Spencer."

"Well, the medal aside, the tabloids have left, and now DICK is on its way out."

"You're kidding."

"No. Yesterday they each got ten tickets for running red lights. The one and only red light camera caught them. Fred spent the past couple hours, tracking them down and suspending their licenses. They said they were innocent, but red light cameras don't lie."

I bit my lip. Red light cameras might not lie, but they didn't recognize that the different license plates were all attached to the same car. A perfect person would have exonerated the DICK people so that they could get their licenses back, but I was slightly less than perfect, and the DICK people annoyed me. It was fitting justice that they would have to take the bus for six months. So, I kept my mouth shut and didn't tell Spencer about Phase Three.

"Now I just have to catch a killer," Spencer said, still smirking. "Notice that I said 'I.' There's no 'you' in 'I.'"

"I'm done," I lied. "I don't want any more dead people on me."

Spencer took my hand and walked into the kitchen. "Sit down," he ordered. I sat down, and he stood over me. "I don't want to scare you."

"You're not scary when you remember to use mouthwash."

"I'm going to ignore that comment for now." He blew into his hand and sniffed to check his breath. "Minty fresh. Listen, Pinky, I want you to stay at home. Fred's coming over, and I'll be home at around three because our couch is being delivered today."

"Why do I need to stay home?"

"Because ever since you started butting your nose in, a killer has been slicing and dicing your father's friends and stuffing them into refrigerators."

So, I wasn't the only one who was scared. "I'm not scared," I said.

He knocked gently on my forehead. "Knock. Knock. Anyone home? There's a killer out there, and you might be next. Stay home until I get back. Okay?"

"Did you talk to Roman and Joy, again?"

"You didn't answer me."

I stuck three fingers up in the air. "Scout's Honor," I said.

For once, I wasn't lying. I didn't have a handle on who did what and why, and I felt like I was flying blind with a big target painted on my braless chest.

"I mean it, Pinky. Stay here with Fred, Meryl, and Zelda."

"Cross my heart, and I don't hope to die."

Spencer studied my face for a minute, probably trying to determine if I was lying. "Pinky, I swear to God, if I find you stuffed in our new refrigerator, I'll be so pissed off."

"We have a new refrigerator?"

I looked over at Grandma's refrigerator. As far as I knew, she had bought it in the 1950s. I was going to miss it. Ditto her table and chairs and linoleum countertops. I was pretty sure there were no linoleum countertops at Spencer's new house.

I mean, *our* new house.

"Our fridge has a special beer section that keeps the beer at the perfect temperature," Spencer said, giddy as a school boy. "The ice cube dispenser has five settings."

It sounded scary, like I wouldn't be able to figure out my own refrigerator. I plastered a phony smile on my face. "Sounds exciting."

Once Fred showed up, Spencer left to return the Bronze Star to old man O'Malley and then to go to work. I installed Fred in the kitchen and gave him a can of cream soda and went upstairs to check on Grandma.

I could hear *Good Morning America* blasting on the television in my grandmother's room through her closed door. I opened it and walked in.

"There you are, girl. Took you long enough." It was Ruth. She was standing next to my grandmother's bed with her hands on her hips. She was wearing her usual no nonsense men's trousers and women's blue button-down shirt. She didn't get along with my grandmother, so I was shocked that she was in her room.

"What are you doing here?" I asked.

"Waiting for you. You're not going to let this refrigerator stuff lie, are you? What would your father say?"

I had no idea what my father would say. I barely knew him. "I don't know what to do," I told her. "I don't have motives. I don't know why Adam and Steve were killed."

"I thought you said she had the Gift, Zelda," Ruth demanded.

"She does have the Gift. Real strong," Grandma said. "Give her a little time. A little space to breathe."

"Okay. But not too much time. Julie is watching Tea Time, so the public's safety is in jeopardy."

"I still don't know what you're doing here," I said.

Ruth took a baseball bat from the corner of the room and held it high. "I brought my Louisville Slugger. I'm going to be your bodyguard, in case someone tries to cut you up and stuff you in a kitchen appliance."

"Ruth, you're a hundred years old. I can hear your knees three minutes before you walk into a room," I pointed out.

"What's your point?"

"Fine. You can be my bodyguard."

She walked around the bed, holding her bat, like she was ready to pound anybody who got too close to me. "What's with the boobies?" she asked. "If you don't wear a bra, your tatas are going to hang to your belly button like two empty socks. You want that? You want two empty socks on your chest?"

CHAPTER 17

Click! Your matches want to click, dolly. I don't know where they heard about this fakakta clicking thing, but you'll hear it all the time. "We just didn't click." or "We clicked!" I don't know what the hell they're talking about. Love is not about clicking. Love is much, much more than clicking. Besides, a match can't be trusted to know if they're clicking or not. A match thinks a little movement in his pants means clicking. But from me to you, a little movement in his pants means a little movement in his pants. It doesn't mean clicking. Yes, there's such a thing as clicking. It's the moment you know that it's right, that everything is the way it should be. But love is a bolt of lightning that hits you between your eyes and changes your life, your mind, and your plans. Know the difference.

Lesson 27, Matchmaking advice from your Grandma Zelda

Ruth shadowed me, not letting me out of her sight, even when I went to my room to put on a bra. "I'm going to start by going through my father's box in the attic," I told her. "You can help. Maybe something will jump out at you."

"I can do that. I know how to read."

We climbed up to the attic, and I was surprised to see Draco, sitting cross-legged on the floor by the window. He was reading an old, yellowed manuscript and eating through a pan of cinnamon buns.

"I'll save you, Gladie!" Ruth yelled as she pushed me out of the way, running with her arthritic legs at poor Draco, her Louisville Slugger ready to knock him to Kingdom Come.

"Stop, Ruth! He's my researcher! He's a kid! He's not the killer!" I yelled. Ruth skidded to a halt, but she kept the bat ready to swing.

"Are you sure? He looks fishy to me."

I swiped the bat from her hands. "He's a kid."

"I'm not a kid," Draco insisted. "I'm a senior in high school."

"Listen, kid. You're a kid," Ruth grumbled.

"What're you doing here? Aren't you supposed to be in school?" I asked him.

Draco stood. "I'm ditching."

"Education's important, young man," I heard myself say. I didn't know what was happening to me. Being around a kid was making me maternal. It was my biggest nightmare.

"I've already been accepted to Stanford, early admission," he explained. "Anyway, this is much more important. I'm reading the best book I've ever read. It's got to be the best book ever written."

He held the manuscript up for us to see, and my breathing stopped. "Did you find that in my father's box?"

"Yep."

Ruth and I exchanged looks. Could it be that my father had written a book that nobody knew about? A fiction book? The best book ever written?

Ruth and I rushed Draco and ripped the manuscript from his hands. I flipped to the title page. My father's name wasn't on it. But Rachel Knight's name was.

"Rachel Knight," I breathed. I had almost forgotten about her. "She died before she could have published this. What a tragedy."

Ruth took the manuscript from me.

"I'm almost done," Draco said. "I've got to find out what happens. It should be made into a movie. May I have it back?"

Ruth wasn't paying attention to him. She had dived into the manuscript, and it had gripped her, too.

"Is it that good?" I asked.

Ruth stopped reading and tried to focus on me. "I've read this book before."

"You have?"

"Half of the world has read this book."

"What are you talking about? Rachel published a book before she died?"

"No. This was published a year after she died. Gladie,

this is Roman Strand's blockbuster, Pulitzer Prize-winning book."

"No fucking way," I breathed.

The three of us pored over Rachel's book. I was one of the few people on the planet who had never read Roman's book, but I knew enough about it to realize that the story was exactly what I was reading in Rachel's manuscript.

"What are you saying?" Draco asked. "Roman Strand is really Rachel Knight? Is he trans or something?"

"Oh, criminy," Ruth complained. "You got into Stanford? What's their selection process these days, drawing straws? No, Roman Strand isn't really Rachel Knight. Roman Strand's book is really Rachel Knight's book!"

Draco's eyes grew big. "The dick. He's rich and famous because he stole some dead girl's book."

"He stole the book," I repeated. "He stole the book. He stole the book."

"You said that, already," Ruth said.

"Rachel Knight killed herself, and then Roman stole her book and got it published," I said.

Ruth whistled. "That's a hell of a timeline."

"I don't get it," Draco said, and Ruth rolled her eyes.

"Rachel Knight killed herself. That's the fishy part."

"I get it, now," Draco said. "Roman Strand killed Rachel Knight and stole her book and became rich and famous. It's like *Game of Thrones* but with writers and no swords."

But there were swords in the form of knives. It made

me wonder how Rachel died. "Draco, would you look up something on the computer?"

Draco worked his magic on my laptop and found out that Rachel Knight died of an overdose of antidepressants and anxiety medication.

"That could be suicide or not suicide," Ruth said, reading my mind. "I have goosebumps, but I don't know why."

I knew why. It was clicking together like puzzle pieces, and as far as I was concerned, the biggest puzzle piece was Roman's book release party. It was all beginning to make sense to me, and it was making me furious.

"Ruth, Rachel Knight didn't kill herself. She was murdered. And I know who killed her and why, and I'm pretty sure I know why Adam and Steve were killed and why, too," I told her.

"It's like watching an episode of *Jessica Jones*," Draco said.

"Come on, Ruth. We gotta go," I said.

"Are we going to bust some ass?"

"I want to come, too," Draco said.

"You can't. It could be dangerous," I explained.

"Do you have a bat?" Ruth asked him. "You can come if you have a bat."

"I'm not very athletic."

Ruth seemed to think about that for a moment. "We might need an extra body, unless you're going to bring the cop, Gladie."

"No cop. Okay, Draco. You can come with us, but stay behind me and if it gets dangerous, run like hell."

"This is so much better than chem class."

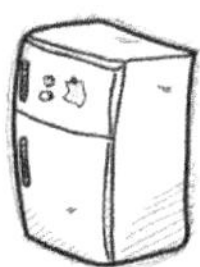

I drove so that Ruth could ride in the passenger seat, holding her bat in case she needed to knock someone's block off. Draco was in the back. We had snuck out without Fred noticing because he was taking a snooze in the parlor.

"We're not going to knock anyone's block off," I told Ruth, even though I knew of one person's block that I wanted to knock.

"Always prepared, Gladie. Always prepared," Ruth said.

"I never knew that old ladies were so kickass," Draco said.

We drove out of the Historic District to Lucy's neighborhood, but we weren't visiting Lucy. I parked a block away from Roman's house. "Nonchalant," I told Ruth and Draco. "Don't draw unwelcome attention."

Ruth opened her door and got out, resting her bat on her shoulder. "No problem. This ain't my first rodeo, you know."

The three of us walked the rest of the way to Roman's house. "Be brave," I told myself and rang the doorbell. Draco picked up a rock while we waited. "What are you doing?"

"I got swept up in the moment," he said.

"No violence," I insisted. "We're here to talk, not to beat anyone up."

"Should I get rid of it?" he asked.

"No. You better keep it," I said and rang the doorbell, again.

Ruth peeked through a window. "I don't think there's anyone home."

Could we be that lucky? "Ruth, keep a lookout while I get us in."

I took my lockpicker's kit out of my purse and went to work.

"Wow, you're a G, Gladie," Draco said.

"I know."

The door opened, and we were in, but the alarm system beeped. I went to the alarm console, but of course, I had no idea what the code was. "Quick, think of a good code," I pleaded.

"One-one-one-one," Ruth suggested.

I tried it, but it didn't work.

"Here, let me try," Draco said, pushing me out of the way. It was impossible. Any amateur thief would tell you that there are ten-thousand combinations in a four-digit code.

Beep, beep, beep, beep. Draco pushed the buttons, and the alarm turned off.

"How did you do that?" I asked.

Draco shrugged. "It was his address. Old people are dumb."

"You're all right for a kid," Ruth told him, patting his back. "Now stay behind me in case the killer jumps out at us and tries to cut you into flank steak."

I searched the house until I found Roman's office. It was wood-paneled and pristine. There wasn't a sign anywhere that he was a writer except for the framed awards and photos of Roman with celebrities and politicians plastered all over the walls. The desk, itself, was totally clean except for a computer. Draco plopped down in Roman's chair and turned the computer on.

"He likes video games," Draco said, typing away on the keyboard. "And porn. Lots of porn. He's a porn king. I've never seen so much porn, and I'm seventeen, so I've seen a lot of porn. It looks like he watches porn about fourteen hours a day."

I gnawed at the inside of my cheek. "Maybe you shouldn't be looking at his computer. I don't know a lot about kids, but I'm pretty sure you're not supposed to be looking at porn."

Draco laughed. "Good one, Gladie. Funny. Nope, there's nothing here about Rachel Knight or the other guys."

"Let's search the rest of the house," I said.

We made our way to the living room and the bedroom. "There's something wrong here," I said, turning around. "Something's not right."

"Did you find the murder weapon?" Ruth asked.

"Did you find body parts?" Draco asked.

"I know what it is," I said. "This is Joy's house."

Ruth furrowed her brow. "Have you had a stroke? You forgot where you are? You're awfully young for a stroke. It's all of that crap food you eat with Zelda. It's probably rotted out half of your insides. Your brain is protesting. It's saying, 'Help! Help!' Would it kill you to eat some All-Bran once in a while? You know, your metabolism isn't going to last forever. You're going to wake up sooner or later and have to be cut out of the side of your house. You think the cop is going to be breathing all hot and heavy when you have a front ass to match your back ass?"

"I know where I am, old woman," I growled. "And what the hell are front and back asses? No, never mind. Don't tell me. I don't need to know. What I'm saying is that this whole mansion belongs to Joy. The only thing she allowed Roman to have is his office, and there's nothing in there of him, either."

"Except for the porn," Draco said.

"Yes, except for the porn."

"That's how it is in a lot of couples' homes," Ruth said. "The woman decorates. The man just watches TV."

Not in Spencer's home. I mean, our home. He was in charge of the decorating; although, he asked me for my opinion every two minutes. "There's no big TV," I said. "No man-style media room."

"She's right," Draco said. "She de-balled him."

"She de-balled him," I repeated, knowing it was true. Then, it hit me. "I know what happened. I know everything."

The sound of the front door opening and closing

reached us. Then, I head Roman and Joy arguing. "I did put the alarm on. I swear it."

"Liar. Don't snivel your way out of this. You were supposed to put the alarm on, and you didn't. Typical. Typical wimp Roman."

The sound of their footsteps came closer. We were cornered in their bedroom, and they were going to find us in a matter of seconds.

"Oh my God, I'm going to be cut up into flank steak," Draco whispered.

"Gladie will save us," Ruth whispered, handing me her bat.

"Me? What about you? You were going to knock their blocks off."

"Get real, Gladie. I'm older than dirt. I'm not going to take out two adults with a baseball bat."

"Fine, then. We're going to die," I said. "Spencer is going to kill me when he finds out I was killed while breaking and entering when I was supposed to stay home. I'll never hear the end of it."

"I'm pretty sure you'll hear the end of it," Ruth said. "Death has a way of doing that."

"I don't want to die," Draco said. "Not like this. Not with old people."

"Would you stop that?" I hissed. "I don't appreciate you talking about age all the time."

"Karma, Gladie. It's a bitch," Ruth said.

"They're coming," Draco said. "Damn it. I left my

rock in the office."

The three of us hugged each other in a huddle, like a football team before a big play. But we had no play planned. Just dying. That was our only plan.

CHAPTER 18

Matchmaking is a lot like a used car dealership. We have the same enthusiasm for beauties that we have for clunkers, because there's no such thing as a match who doesn't deserve to love and be loved. She could be a mieskeit with a face that could stop traffic or a zeisgeit with a body who could stop time. Either way, we sell love. Not illegal, red light kind of love. Real, happy ending love. But like the used car salesmen, sometimes we have to do a hard sell and sometimes a soft sell. With a soft sell, we ease a match into her happily ever after. With a hard sell, we do a big push. Pushing isn't easy, bubbeleh. No nice person wants to be pushy. We want it all to flow naturally. But from time to time, you're going to have to push and you're going to have to push HARD. Don't be afraid. Don't be shy. Push! Attack! Go get 'em!

Lesson 132, Matchmaking advice from your Grandma Zelda

"Hurry! Into the bathroom!" I hissed. We ran into the bathroom with Ruth pushing her way in front of Draco and me. "There's no lock. What kind of crazy people don't have a lock on the bathroom door? What if someone walks in when they're pooping?"

"Focus, Gladie," Ruth said. "We're about to be fileted. Why are you thinking about pooping?"

"I don't know about you, but I'm going to poop my pants," Draco said. "I think it's called being scared shitless."

"Be quiet," I mouthed. "Find a weapon."

Draco picked up a razor and I went for the curtain rod. If it got bad, I could impale them with it. As quietly as I could, I pushed aside the shower curtain and was thrilled to discover there was a good-sized window.

"Let's get the hell out of here," I mouthed.

"What did you say?" Ruth asked.

"Shh!"

I opened the window, which was high up on the wall. "Alley oop," I told Ruth.

"Very funny. I can't get up there."

"Okay. Draco and I will heave-ho you up and through the window."

Ruth pursed her lips. "A broken hip is a death sentence to a woman my age, you know."

"Would you rather be cut into bite-sized pieces and stuffed into a refrigerator?" I asked.

"You have a point," she said. "Go ahead. Heave-ho me."

It wasn't easy to heave-ho her. She wasn't the most flexible of people and I wasn't the strongest. Draco and I linked hands under Ruth's butt and lifted her. Once she got her hands on the window ledge, we pushed and pushed until she fell through to the other side with a loud *oomph.*

"I may be dead," I heard her moan.

"I'm outta here," Draco announced and flew through the window like he had wings.

"Sonofabitch," Ruth moaned. "Did you have to land on me?"

"Why didn't you move out of the way?" Draco complained.

"Because I'm older than your great-grandmother, and I just fell out of a window."

"I got bush in my eye. My eye!" Draco yelled.

I gripped the windowsill and tried to pull myself up, but I didn't have any upper body strength. I had never managed to do a pull up in my entire life. There was no way I was going to get through the window. It was impossible. I would never ever manage to climb through it.

Behind me, the doorknob turned and the door began to open. Suddenly, I was imbued with superhuman strength. I pulled myself up. Right before I ducked through the window, I turned to see Roman enter the bathroom and give me a threatening glare.

I sailed through the window and landed hard on my knee in a bush, right before Ruth rolled out of the way. Draco helped me up and we both helped Ruth up.

"Run like the wind!" I yelled.

We hung on to each other for support with Ruth in the middle. With her hurt hip, Ruth hobbled. With my hurt knee, I had to hop on one foot, and Draco just needed guidance, since he was half-blind.

"Unless they're running after us in quicksand, there's no way we're going to outrun them," Ruth said.

She was totally right. "You're wrong, Ruth," I said. "It's just a matter of attitude. We can outrun them."

"Between the three of us, we have four good legs and five eyes. We're doomed," she said wisely.

"We'll outwit them," I told her. "Make a left at the hedges and a right at the creek. They won't find us."

He didn't find us. We made it back to the car. I drove us back into the Historic District, using my left foot for the pedals because my right knee was killing me.

"I have a busted hip and I'll never get my Louisville Slugger back," Ruth complained.

"Do you think I'll lose my eye?" Draco asked. "Will I need an eye patch?"

"You're both going to be totally fine. We're just bruised a little. Take a shower and a couple Advil and you'll be right as rain."

"I think my hip bone went through my pelvis," Ruth

said. "I'm pregnant with my hip bone. I've become a carnival act."

"Do girls like eye patches?" Draco asked.

I couldn't get through Main Street to Tea Time because it was packed with people, celebrating in the street. "What's going on?"

"This must be the resistance celebration," Draco said. "I've been out of touch, but we were going to party once DICK was chased out of town."

"I heard that all of the DICK people had their driver's licenses suspended," I said.

"Phase Three," Draco said. "It worked better than the bubble gum."

"I'm still finding bubble gum in every nook and cranny at Tea Time," Ruth said.

"Collateral damage," Draco said. "Couldn't be helped. The ends justify the means."

"Is that what they're going to teach you at Stanford?" Ruth asked. "You majoring in Ayn Rand? Perfect. Another spoiled, middle-American male, bowing at the altar of *Atlas Shrugged*. Just what this country needs."

"You don't like the DICK people either, Ruth," I pointed out.

"Yes, but just because they're Nazis doesn't mean that I get so nutso that I make the town miserable. Collateral damage? Shame on you, kid. Shame on you. If I have problems with them, I tell them in a mature, calm way."

I parked about four blocks from Tea Time and we

hobbled, limped, and stumbled our way down the street. Teenagers were whooping it up, throwing confetti, and dancing to music I had never heard before. It took us twenty minutes to walk the four blocks and that's when we saw the charter busses. A long line of cardigan-wearing people were waiting to board and they didn't look happy about it.

Defeat.

I knew it well.

A group of teenagers were sticking their tongues out at the line of cardigans and calling them horrible names. At least I thought they were horrible names. I had never heard the words before. I guessed I really was getting old, since I didn't recognize the teenagers' language or their music.

"This town is damned!" one DICK member shouted, unable to handle the teenagers' jeers for one more second.

Another cardigan-wearer pointed in our direction, singling out Ruth. "Her! She's the dildo woman! She started this!"

"She cursed the town with her indecency, spreading it to the youth!" another DICK member shouted about Ruth.

Draco and I were each supporting Ruth, as she stood between us with her arms around our shoulders. I felt her tense and she was breathing hard, like a bull ready to charge.

"Remember you're mature and calm," I said.

"Shut up, Gladie. Nobody's mature and calm around Nazis," she said and ordered us to walk her across the street to face her accusers.

"Look what you've done to this town," one of the

DICK men spat at Ruth. "Look at the youth. They're wild heathens!"

Holding onto Draco and me, Ruth stood as straight as she could and narrowed her eyes. "Listen to me, you two-bit Eichmann wannabe. Where you see wild heathens, I see young people with a true understanding of what it means to live in a free society and their responsibility to participate in civil disobedience in order to maintain that free society. You wouldn't understand democracy if it bit you on your bony ass. If our town has to scrape some bubble gum off the benches, it's worth it if it means ridding Cannes of your invading species of mold that has tried to creep its way into our souls, trying to turn them into diseased, gangrenous mounds of putrefaction...just like your souls. If you even have souls. So, you leave the young people of Cannes alone. They are the best this world has to offer. They are the generation of hope and promise. They will not be silenced and their growth will not be stunted. Not by the likes of you cardigan-wearing know-it-all prudes. As for me, if I want to own every dildo on the planet, I will. In fact, I might start selling them next to my collection of hand-crocheted tea cozies and I might even change the name of my shop to Dildos-R-Us. Be gone, you low-life, vanilla bean, melba toast excuse for human beings!"

The teenagers had become quiet during Ruth's tirade. When she finally finished, they erupted in applause and cheers and lifted her into the air, as if it was a mosh pit at an outdoor concert. "Let me down, you heathens!" she shouted at them. “You good for nothing teenagers, let me down! My hip! You’re killing me!”

“I’ll help her,” Draco announced and ran after her as she was tossed from teenager to teenager down the street.

My phone rang and I answered it while the charter buses roared to life and the DICK people quickly finished getting on board. “Hello?”

“Gladie, darlin’, you wouldn’t believe the day I’m having.”

Draco ran after Ruth and disappeared into the crowd, but the teenagers were tossing Ruth faster than Draco could run. The charter buses finally left, thankfully going in the opposite direction.

“Are you having a bad day?” I asked Lucy.

“Well, I came back rested and refreshed from the spa, but that stupid Italian chef that Harry rented gave me a hard time. Now I have knots in my neck the size of softballs, because of the stress.”

“That’s terrible,” I said, adjusting my weight off of my knee, which had swollen so much that it was pushing against the material of my track suit.

“You know what that pasta cooker accused me of, Gladie? He said I stole from him. Let me say that again, because I’m sure you didn’t understand it. He said that I…stole…from…him.”

“He did? That’s crazy. Aren’t you paying him a fortune? What did he say you stole?”

“Two knives. I guess they’re special kinds of knives

from Germany, but who is he kidding? Why would I steal knives? The last time I cooked was twenty-three years ago when I made macaroni and cheese out of a box."

Through the crowd, I saw Roman coming my way. We locked eyes and he sped up, walking in my direction. Oh, crap. I had to get out of there fast. Luckily, Roman was slowed down by the crowd. I didn't have much time to make my escape.

"Lucy, I'll call you right back," I said and hung up. I hopped away as fast as I could, taking the side streets on my way home.

It wouldn't be hard for Roman to find out where I lived, but Fred was at my grandmother's house and he could protect me. I could also call the police, but all I could tell them was that while I was breaking and entering, Roman scared me with a mean look. Besides, the police were busy trying to maintain peace in the Historic District.

I hid in the bushes a couple houses down from my grandmother's and looked out for Roman. There was no sign of him. I was sure he would find me eventually, but for now I had out-hopped him and was in the clear.

My knee was worse and it took me forever to hobble the rest of the distance to my grandmother's house. Across the street, the construction workers were gone for the day, but a truck had parked in the driveway and two men were carrying out something large.

"Careful! Careful!" Spencer shouted at them. "That's a custom-made couch!"

"We know. We built it," one of the men said.

Spencer continued to order them around. "That's right. You got it. A little to the left. Now a little to the right."

"This isn't our first delivery job, you know," one of the men said.

I limped across the street. Spencer was happy to see me, assuming that I was coming from Grandma's house. "Look, Pinky. Our couch has arrived. Come on in and see how it looks in our house."

Spencer was like a kid on Christmas Day and Santa Claus had given him his own bag of presents. He was so excited that he didn't recognize that I was injured. We followed the delivery men into the house. Spencer barked orders at them to put the couch in just the right place. They removed the plastic from the couch and Spencer inspected the fabric to make sure it was in perfect shape. When he was finally satisfied, he shook the delivery men's hands and let them leave.

Spencer wrapped his arms around me. "Doesn't the couch look wonderful in our beautiful home?"

"It does," I said truthfully.

"The television will be on this wall." He pointed at the wall opposite the couch. "Can't you just see us in the evenings, cuddling on the couch, watching TV next to a roaring fire in the fireplace?"

"That sounds nice."

"We're going to get every channel. I found a satellite dish company that offers three hundred more channels than its closest competitor."

"I'll never stop watching TV. It sounds perfect."

"The house is really coming along. Don't you think so, Pinky?"

"It's beautiful." All of the major renovations were done and it looked nothing like the cursed house that I had known for the past year. I could almost forget about the death and destruction I had witnessed in the house. Perhaps the love between Spencer and me could erase all of that. Perhaps the house was no longer cursed. "I love the house, Spencer. Really."

"I think we're going to be very happy here, Pinky. If you don't spill anything on the couch."

"I'll put a towel down before I sit on it."

"Promise?"

"Promise."

Spencer arched an eyebrow and smirked his little smirk. "You know, we're alone in the house. Just you and me. We could get down and dirty in total privacy."

"On the couch?"

"Pinky, the couch is sacred. But the carpeting is extra plush." He kissed my neck. "Please, Pinky. Play naked with me on the carpet."

"Okay. I guess so."

He smiled wide and hopped excitedly on his heels. "I've got champagne in the wine cooler. I'll go get it."

"You have a wine cooler?"

"No, *we* have a wine cooler."

Spencer ran to the kitchen, and I sat down on the couch. It was crazy comfortable. Grandma's furniture in her parlor was at least thirty years old and the cushions had worn thin. But Spencer's couch was plush, even more comfortable than my bed.

There was a crash in the kitchen. "Uh oh," I called. "Did the champagne bite it? That's okay. I'll play naked with you for a 7Up. I'm easy, but don't let it get around. Spencer?"

He didn't respond. I stood up, and that's when I saw them. Roman and Joy walked into the living room and Roman was aiming a gun at me.

"Did you hurt Spencer?" I started to cry, big tears falling down my cheeks, thinking that Spencer was hurt. Or worse.

"Why couldn't you leave well enough alone?" Roman asked. "Your father was dead for years and everyone was happy. But you had to stir the pot. It's your fault."

"Is Spencer okay?"

"And you had to get Adam and Steve involved. You must have known how that was going to end."

"No. How would I have known?" I said, looking alternately at Roman's gun and watching to see if Spencer was on his way to save me. "When I came to you, I didn't know a thing about Rachel Knight. I didn't know that you murdered her and stole her manuscript." Roman's chin dropped to his chest and he took a deep breath.

"You may be a terrible writer, but you knew a good book when you read it," I continued. "It was good enough to kill for. Well, that's obvious because it made you rich and famous, not to mention all of the awards. It set you up for the rest of your life. Your life and Joy's life."

"Don't say a word, Roman," Joy said. "She doesn't know anything."

"That was the puzzle piece that I was missing," I continued. "I couldn't figure out the murders, my father's death, until I found out about Rachel and her book. Then, it was easy to put the puzzle together. Once I knew about that, the release party made sense."

"What are you talking about?" Joy asked.

"Shut up," Roman told her.

"You were so excited at your big book release party," I said to Roman. "So excited that it didn't even dawn on you that Rachel might have shown my father her manuscript."

"She told me that the book was a secret, that she had only shown it to me. I didn't know that she showed it to Jonathan," Roman said.

"Shut up, Roman," Joy commanded.

"What does it matter now?" he asked.

"Rachel had shown the book to my father," I said. "Just like Adam had shown him *Fart Boy*. So, when you proudly gave my father a signed copy of your newly published book, he was happy for you until he read it. Then, I'm guessing it clicked for him pretty fast. He knew you stole the book from Rachel and it wasn't a big leap to figure out that you had killed her. He called you and set up a time to talk. You knew what that conversation was going to be about and you decided that you couldn't let him spread the word."

"Be careful, Roman," Joy said.

"Why should he be careful, Joy?" I asked. "Because you don't want him to tell me that you're the one who killed my father? I already know that, Joy. Being in your house told me everything I needed to know. Your house. Your belongings. Roman's prison. This is what I'm thinking happened: You found out that Roman killed Rachel and stole her book and you decided to help him for a price. You caused my father's accident and made all of Roman's problems disappear. And the price? Roman had to marry you. He did and he's paid for it since then. Roman, when you first showed me the wreckage of my father's motorcycle in your garage, I was suspicious. I thought that you had kept it, because it was your way to laud your success over my father's head, even if the only thing left of my father was that lump of twisted metal. But now I know the real reason you kept the bike."

"Why?" Joy asked.

"Don't you know?" I asked. "He kept it to hold over you. Blackmail. If you ratted him out, he would rat you out. It didn't make his life any better, but it was the small window of freedom in the prison that you had built for him. It's funny that Roman got everything that every writer dreams of: riches, acclaim, and the world at his feet. But it didn't change the fact that he lived every day under your thumb and in fear that you were going to let the world know that he was a fraud. And then it got worse."

"It got worse because of you," Joy said. "You stuck

your nose in. I had heard about you. Nosey Parker. Buttinski. Yenta. You've caused a lot of trouble for a lot of people."

"I've been told it's a gift," I said.

"Your gift got two people killed. After today, four people."

My heart thumped in my chest. There was still no sign of Spencer and I had no idea how to get out of this mess.

"I loved your father," Roman told me. "He was my best friend."

"And you didn't want Adam and Steve to die either," I said. "But you could have saved them. You could have stopped Joy."

"No, I couldn't. You don't understand who she is. I can't stop her."

"You chose not to stop her," I insisted. "All this blood is on your hands."

"This has been fun, but we need to wrap it up," Joy said and took a knife out of her purse.

"The Italian's chef's knife," I said. "He's missing a couple of them and I figure that all you rich people rent the same chefs. He must have cooked at your house at some point and you stole his knives."

"He makes good fresh pasta," Joy said and, without another word, she came at me with the knife. I stumbled backward and my knee gave out, making me fall onto the couch. She slashed wildly and I rolled out of her reach. The knife made contact with the couch over and over, cutting it into shreds, but I couldn't evade her knife forever.

I screamed when her knife made contact with my arm. She tried to stab me again, but this time I managed to block her and flip her onto her back. She wrenched free of me and stabbed wildly again. Luckily, she missed me, hitting the sofa again. I rolled off the couch and tried to get up and make my escape, but my knee wouldn't cooperate. Roman waved the gun at me.

"You can't leave. I'll have to shoot you," he said.

But he was wrong. Spencer took that moment to show up. His head was a bloody mess. The blood had run down his face and he wiped it out of his eyes right before he pistol whipped Roman on the back of his head, making him crumple to the ground in an unconscious heap.

I tried to crawl away to safety, away from Joy, but she came after me with her knife. "Stop, or I'll shoot!" Spencer yelled.

"No, you won't," Joy yelled, grabbing me from behind and putting the knife to my throat.

Spencer shot his gun, hitting Joy's knife hand. She fell backward onto the couch. The knife flew out of her hand and landed deep into the couch.

"Are you okay, Pinky?" Spencer asked.

"Yes. I hurt my knee and she stabbed my arm. How about you?" He whimpered and his eyes filled with tears. "What's the matter? Is it your head? Are you going to die? Spencer, please tell me."

"My couch," he cried. "She killed my beautiful couch."

CHAPTER 19

Your matches are looking for their happy endings. Their happily ever afters. The thing is that happy endings are just the beginning. They represent a life change, which will change your matches in ways they never expected. But you need to expect the changes, bubbeleh. A matchmaker needs to know what will happen after the ending…when the beginning will happen.

Lesson 118, Matchmaking advice from your Grandma Zelda

Spencer got thirty stitches in his head. I got fourteen stitches in my arm. Spencer had a concussion, so I had to wake him up in the middle of the night and ask him who the president was. I was given good drugs for my knee and a brace to wear for a couple weeks.

Spencer arrested Roman and Joy and handed them over to Remington and Margie, while we went to the hospital. As soon as we were released, I went home, sat on Grandma's bed, held her hand, and told her the truth about her son's death.

We cried about the senseless loss of a beautiful and loved man. We celebrated the truth that he was willing to stand up for his friend, Rachel, and confront Roman. And we breathed. Closure was good for breathing, but it didn't necessarily help with grief. The sadness was still there. The loss was still keenly felt. But we felt closer to my father, knowing why he died and knowing about the last days of his life.

It turned out that Ruth's hip was only bruised, and Draco's cornea was scratched but would be fine. Even though Draco was another spoiled, middle-American male, bowing at the altar of *Atlas Shrugged*, Ruth gave him a part-time job at Tea Time, washing tea cups.

I had started this journey in the attic, thinking that my father was alive. That didn't turn out to be the case, but at least he got some justice. With the chapter of my father's death closed, a certain amount of serenity settled on my grandmother's house, while Spencer and I slept on and off for three days.

"My poor couch," he moaned on the third day, as we lay in each other's arms in my bed. "It never did anything to anyone. It didn't even live long enough to have a butt mark. My butt never touched it. Poor couch."

"I'm so sorry," I said, feeling responsible for the loss of his beloved couch. "What can I do to make you feel better?"

"Nothing. Not unless you have a custom-made couch hidden somewhere for me."

"I don't have a couch. How about I let you do that thing to me that I've always refused to do?"

Spencer sat up in bed. "Really? The thing that I really want to do, but you said that Jewish girls weren't allowed to do or they would turn into salt?"

"Yes, that's the one."

"Is it my birthday, or am I dying, and you're keeping it secret from me?"

"Spencer, I'm sorry about your couch. I mean our couch. I want you to know that I appreciate you making a home for us. I know you're doing it because you love me."

"I do love you, Pinky. And I'll love you even more when we do the thing."

"You've been so considerate, trying to make a perfect house for me with every thoughtful detail. I don't think I've shown you how much I appreciate everything that you do."

"Letting me do the thing will show me your appreciation."

"Okay. Okay. Let's do the thing." My phone rang.

"Don't answer that," Spencer urged. "Call them back after we do the thing."

"I have to answer. It's Bridget. What if she's in labor?"

"She's always in labor. C'mon, Pinky. Do a guy a favor. I'm in mourning over my couch."

I answered the phone. "Bridget? Are you okay?"

"You better come over quick, Gladie. *Oooouuuuahhhh*!!!"

"I'll be right there!"

Bridget didn't come to her door, so I let myself in with the extra key she had given me. I found her sitting at her kitchen table with her knees together and a layer of sweat on her face.

"Make it stop, Gladie," she whimpered.

I mopped her face with a napkin and gave her a glass of water. "How are you feeling, Bridget? Do you want to go to the hospital? Should I call Dr. Sara?"

"No. We can't. I can't have the baby, Gladie."

"Why not? Is something wrong?"

"He doesn't like me."

"Who doesn't like you?"

"My baby. He doesn't like me."

"He loves you," I assured her.

"No, he doesn't. That's why he hasn't wanted to come out. It's because he doesn't like me."

I held Bridget's hands and looked her in the eyes. "Bridget Donovan, you are my best friend in the whole world. You are the sweetest, kindest, most empathetic person I've ever met. Your son is the luckiest little boy to have a mother like you. He's going to like you. He's going to adore you. Are you in labor?"

"My water broke an hour ago."

"Okay. Let's get going and welcome this beautiful little boy into the world."

I called Dr. Sara and told her to meet us. At the hospital, the nurses seemed to understand that this time, Bridget was really and truly in labor. Bridget was strangely calm, and so was I. It might have been because we had had so many practice drills that when the real moment happened, it was anti-climactic.

"Alexa, Debussy," Dr. Sara ordered when Bridget was ready to push after a few hours of labor. It only took her three pushes to bring her baby into the world. Dr. Sara let me cut the umbilical cord, and she handed the baby to Bridget. It was the most powerful experience of my life. Seeing Bridget's son born filled me with emotion.

"He's so beautiful," I blubbered. "Look what you did. You made a human being. You're a miracle worker. You're amazing."

"I made a human being," Bridget repeated, looking into the eyes of her son.

"Feel his skin. It's so soft. I exfoliate, but my skin doesn't feel anything like this. What a cutie pie. Little Fidel, or is it Lech or Che? What did you name him?" I asked.

"His name is Jonathan."

My throat grew thick, and I cried some more. "You named him after my father?"

Bridget took my hand and gave it a squeeze. "I

couldn't think of a better man to name my son after."

I stayed with Bridget and little Jonathan for a few hours until Bridget fell asleep and the nurses shooed me out of the hospital. I was exhausted. Not only was the labor long, but it was emotional. On the way home, I stopped at Tea Time for coffee.

I opened the door to the tea shop. It was practically empty. Ruth was sitting at a table with another woman, and they were the only ones in the place. "Ruth, latte," I ordered, as I walked inside.

"Cool your jets, girl. Can't you see that I'm busy?" she said.

"I just helped bring life into the world. I need coffee, Ruth."

As I reached the table where Ruth was sitting, I stopped cold in my tracks. I rubbed my eyes, unsure that I was seeing what I thought I was seeing. The woman sitting with Ruth was an old lady, dressed in a Vera Wang knockoff.

"Grandma?" I asked. "Is that you?"

"Of course, dolly. Who else would it be?" she said.

Normally, it would be anybody except for my grandmother. Grandma hadn't left her property line willingly since my father died years ago. "What are you doing here?" I asked.

"I'm having a nice cup of tea and a bran muffin. Beautiful day, don't you think, bubbeleh? Perfect day for new beginnings."

THE END

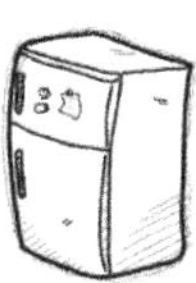

Check out the next installment with *It's a Wonderful Knife. Keep reading for a preview of this book!*

And don't forget to sign up for the newsletter for new releases and special deals: https://bit.ly/2PzAhRx

IT'S A WONDERFUL KNIFE EXCERPT

CHAPTER 1

My grandfather died when I was a little girl. I don't remember much about him, but he was a big man, and he never came downstairs before he was fully dressed in a pressed suit, tie, and pocket square. And then he was dead. The day after his funeral, I was in my grandmother's bathroom, which is my bathroom now, and there he was. Big and dressed in his best suit, he was staring back at me in the mirror. As you can imagine, I didn't say a word to him, and he didn't say a word to me. Probably because he was dead. But even when he was alive, he didn't say a word to me. So, it wasn't a big, loving reunion scene or anything, bubbeleh. He stared at me in the mirror, and after a few seconds, I turned around to see if he was in the room. Bupkes. He wasn't there. When I turned back to the mirror, he was still watching me with a blank expression on his face. He was probably as surprised to see me as I was to see him. After all, I had no business being in my Grandma's bathroom. I was pretty stoic as a little girl, but sharing a bathroom with a dead man blew through my calm demeanor. I screamed like a meshuganah. Grandma came running, and so did my mother. My grandfather disappeared before they arrived, but my mother and grandmother believed me when I told them that I had been visited by an apparition. They both spit to ward against the evil eye, and then they told me the secret of love, right there between the toilet and the tub. They explained that only love can make spirits move between worlds, because love isn't part of the physical world or the spiritual world. Love is its own world, a mystical force that adopts us or leaves us on a whim, like a cat. The more we open our hearts, the more chance we have of possessing love in our lives. There was also this, and it's probably the most important thing: The more you give, the more you get. It's the karma of love and it's not always immediate, but eventually—eventually—love comes to the loving. Be loving. Promote love. Be loved. I love you, dolly.

Lesson 3, Matchmaking advice from your Grandma Zelda

So, this was how it happened when everything was going right. Love life… right. Career… right. Hair…right. Deluxe super fancy latte maker machine in new custom-built house… right. Rockabilly band for impending wedding… right. Everything, every aspect of my life, was going right. And what normally happens in cases like this when everything a person has ever wanted—and even the things she didn't know she wanted—have come true, is that they become a serene, enlightened, sublimely happy person who can out-cool the Dalai Lama and even give up blinking.

So funny. As if.

In reality, I had everything I wanted and everything I didn't know I wanted, and I was freaking the shit out.

It might have been because I was in charge of the Sunday Singles meeting, since my grandmother was MIA, but I was betting it was more likely worrying about Eileen the street sweeper singing Ave Maria at my wedding.

My. Wedding.

It never dawned on me that what I thought was my happily ever after was only a transition to my real happily ever after.

"Where's Zelda?" Sally Salken asked. We were sitting on folding chairs in a circle in the parlor, and I was sensing a certain amount of doubt in my abilities from Cannes' singles.

"I think she's ice skating," I said. Since Grandma had started leaving her property line, she was never home. She had been a shut-in since my father died years ago, but since we discovered the truth about his death, she was undergoing a rebirth. She had always been a social butterfly, but now the butterfly was flying all over the place.

"It's July. Who goes ice skating in July?" Sally Salken

said.

"She said something about a rink in San Diego next to a churro stand," I said.

"Soon there'll be no ice skating because the earth is getting closer to the sun," Jenny Jackson explained. "That's called global warming."

"There's no such thing as global warming," Millicent Lane spat. "Everyone knows that when the earth gets closer to the sun, the sun backs up. That way the earth stays the same, temperature-wise. We're just at the time right before the sun takes a few steps backward."

"That doesn't sound right to me," Jenny said.

"I saw it on PBS," Millicent insisted.

"Since when do you watch PBS?" Sally demanded.

"Ruth Fletcher made me put it on the TV when she came in for a cleaning."

Millicent was the town's new dental hygienist, and Ruth Fletcher was the ornery tea shop owner, who would have flailed Millicent alive if she had heard her theory about global warming.

"Anyway, today's talk is about preparing for happiness," I said.

"Preparing? I'm ready," Sally announced, and everyone laughed.

"Sometimes, we don't know what happiness is, what will actually make us happy," I said. "We're trying for something, going down a path toward it, but it's not the thing that will really make us happy."

"This is depressing. Zelda never makes us depressed," Jenny complained.

My forehead broke out in sweat, and it got pretty wet between my breasts, too. Flop sweat. I knew it well. Grandma was having fun, eating churros while she ice-skated, but in her absence, I had to take up the slack and was stuck with every group meeting and volunteer organization committee. And I wasn't the best at any of it. Sure, I had gotten better since I had moved into town to help my grandmother with her matchmaking business, but I was no Zelda Burger. There was only one of her, and I wasn't it, no matter how many times she told me I had the gift.

"Sorry," I said. "I didn't mean to depress you. What I mean is that we have to prepare for happiness and really understand what's in our heart."

"How do we do that?" Sally asked.

"Vision boards," I said.

Millicent clapped her hands. "I love arts and crafts!"

I hated arts and crafts. I couldn't even draw a stick figure. But I had to make a showing with the vision boards, or nobody would come to me to be matched. I refused to be the downfall of Zelda's Matchmaking while she was having fun in San Diego. So, I had woken up early in the morning and drove to Walley's, where I bought poster boards, arts and crafts supplies, and a pile of magazines to use for pictures. Luckily, my grandmother had left me with a debit card for expenses. I had never felt so rich in my life. I even bought Crayola brand markers instead of the generic kind.

"Crayola," I announced and pointed to them, like I was wearing a spangly dress on *The Price is Right*. I laid out all the supplies on the dining room table, and the women went right to work.

"This is great," Sally said, cutting out pictures of Chris Pine from People magazine. "I know someone who did a vision board, and three weeks later she won the lottery."

"I'd love a George Clooney lottery," Millicent said. "He gets my juices flowing."

They cut and pasted. They drew little flowers and glittered everything. My vision board was blank. I didn't know what to do with it.

"Look, Gladie's board is blank," Sally said. "Of course it is. She already has the perfect man, and he's building her the perfect house."

"Yes," I said. "That's true."

But I still felt like my vision board needed something different. Something new. My grandmother had planned most of my wedding, but it was up to me to pick Spencer's wedding gift. He was the best dressed man of our town, Cannes. He had a designer wardrobe, and he now had a designer house, which was almost done. What could I get for him? What item would illustrate my love for him?

I picked up the special edition Burnt Sienna Crayola marker and drew a large question mark in the center of my board.

"Oh, that's deep, Gladie," Jenny said, studying my question mark. "What do you think about my Mercedes? Too much?"

"Not at all," I said. "I mean, if you think a Mercedes will make you happy."

She studied her glittery vision board. "It wouldn't make me *un*happy."

She had a point. I didn't think a Mercedes would make anyone unhappy. My friend Lucy had a Mercedes with seat warmers, and she was very happy.

Fifteen minutes later, the class was over. "No class next Sunday," I announced. "I'll see you all in two weeks."

"You mean you'll see us in one week," Millicent corrected. "We've all been invited to your wedding."

"You have?" I asked, surprised. Her face dropped, and I cleared my throat. "I mean, of course you have." It was a sad attempt at covering my slight, but she accepted it.

"I'm wearing a blue and white sundress," she told me, excitedly. "I love that you're having an outside wedding. You're going to have single men there, right?"

"Of course."

I had no idea who was going to be there. I suspected the whole town was going to be there. I didn't even know it was an outside wedding.

My stomach growled. There was leftover lasagna in the refrigerator, but desperate times called for fries and a chocolate shake. "I'll walk you out," I told the women and grabbed my purse.

They left the house holding their vision boards, imbued with renewed optimism that their fantasies and wishes would come true. A blast of hot air hit us when I opened the front door.

Sally groaned. "One-hundred-two today."

"We're in a pineapple, that's why. I heard it on the news," Millicent explained.

"The pineapple is the rain. We're in a pocket," Jenny said. "A pocket with a zipper that's closed tight, so the heat can't escape."

We were back to a scientific conversation that had no basis in reality. But one thing was certain. It was hot. I was wearing cutoffs, a tank top, and flip-flops, and I was sweating two seconds after I left my grandmother's air-conditioned house.

"It is called a pineapple," Millicent insisted. "And it's going to get worse. A super pineapple. That's what we're going to have. Sorry, Gladie. I hope your wedding won't be ruined."

Watching the Sunday Singles get in their cars and drive away, I worried that my wedding would be ruined. I pictured walking down the aisle with big fat sweat stains under my arms and my hair frizzed out, just like it was now. I had tried to tame it with a lot of product and a ponytail, but my hair had a life of its own, and it was escaping the ponytail elastic in long frizzy tendrils.

Across the street, a couple of workers were walking in and out of the house. The renovations were almost done. Spencer had pulled out all the stops to make it gorgeous, and I still couldn't believe that I was going to move into it after my wedding on Sunday. There was a Jacuzzi attached to the pool in the backyard, and there was another Jacuzzi tub and steam room in the master bath.

With all of those Jacuzzis, I would never have to worry about a sore muscle again. "How the hell did I get here?" I asked aloud and opened my car door.

Luckily, my Cutlass Supreme had killer air conditioning. I blasted it and turned on the radio to the oldies station. I drove through the historic district on my way to Burger Boy. The town was pretty quiet, and I assumed that most of the townspeople were hiding from the heat.

Then, I saw a ruckus on the sidewalk on Main Street, next to the pharmacy. The mayor was waving his arms at a man in a military uniform. I couldn't hear them, but I could tell that it was a screaming match.

The mayor was wearing a white linen suit, and he seemed no match for the military guy with thick epaulets and a chest covered in medals. I didn't have time to wonder what the argument was about because I had a milkshake with my name on it, waiting for me.

Even though it was hotter than hell, it was a gorgeous day. There wasn't a cloud in the sky, and the mountain was lush and green. Burger Boy was by the lake, and if I had been at all athletic, I would have rented one of the paddle boats or kayaks they offered at the lake and made a day of it.

But I wasn't athletic.

I turned into the Burger Boy driveway and stopped at the large Burger Boy plastic head to order. Opening my window, I shouted into the head. "I'll have the double Burger Boy with cheese, large fries, and chocolate milkshake, no whipped cream. Oh, what the hell. Yes, I'll take the whipped cream. Hello? Hello?"

Nothing. And the window was open, bringing gusts of hot air into the car.

"Hello?" I tried again.

"The head don't work, like, you know?" a voice said. I craned my head to see a familiar-looking skateboarder.

"Oh, dude, it's you," he said. "Hey, dudes, look, it's the babe!" he shouted.

There was the sound of wheels on pavement, and then his three skateboarding friends rolled up to the car.

"Did you ever get away from that harsh killer bitch?" one of the skateboarders asked me.

They had helped me when I was running away from a killer nearly a year before. "Yes, that was almost a year ago."

"Cool."

"Yeah, cool."

"Cool, dude."

"How have you been?" I asked them.

"Like, you know," one of them answered. He was wearing board shorts and a t-shirt with *What country would Jesus bomb?* written in purple neon on it.

"Hangin'," another clarified.

"Hangin'," the others repeated.

"Can you spare a buck for a milkshake?" one asked me. Grandma's debit card burned a hole in my pocket. They were a bunch of potheads, but they weren't bad guys. It was the least I could do to buy them milkshakes.

"Sure. Let me park."

I parked by the door to the restaurant and got out. The skateboarders hopped onto the sidewalk and flipped their boards up and caught them.

"Cool," one of them said.

"Cool," the others repeated in unison.

"Cool," I said because I didn't know what else to say. They were all high, or they had smoked so much pot in their lives that they were permanently stoned.

"Oh, dude, look at that," one of them said pointing to the telephone pole over Burger Boy. There was an owl flapping its wings, but it was attached to the pole and seemed distressed. I couldn't believe my eyes.

"It's plastic," I explained.

"Cool. It's like a real kind of plastic."

"Yeah, real kind of plastic."

"You know, pot isn't good for your brain," I said.

"Weed is life. Weed is legal."

"Weed is legal."

"Like, it's a plant, dude."

"Like, a plant."

"Cool."

"Yeah, cool."

"Oh, dude, the plastic bird. Dude."

"Dude."

I looked up, again. The owl was flapping in obvious

distress. "I think it's a robot," I said, gnawing at the inside of my cheek.

About a year ago, I had mistaken a plastic owl for a real one at this very spot, and the result was humiliating and life-threatening. There was no way I was going to fall for that, again.

The owl started to screech, loudly.

"Cool robot," one of the skateboarders said.

"I'm not falling for this, again," I said. "Somebody go up there and help it."

They stared at me and didn't say anything. I figured their drug-addled brains were trying to figure out what to say.

"I know. I'll call for help this time. Nine-one-one works, now." But in my hurry to get a milkshake, I had forgotten my cellphone on the kitchen table. "One of you call for help," I told them.

"My mom took my phone, dude. She said I was wasting my life."

"I lost mine at the pool."

"I took mine into the pool. Dude, phones should work in the pool."

"Dude."

"Yeah, dude."

The owl screeched and flapped its wings, as if it was panicked. If it wasn't helped soon, it would break its leg or worse.

"I cannot believe this is happening," I said and put my purse down on the sidewalk. "How is it possible to do this twice in one lifetime?" I grabbed the metal handles and pulled myself up. "Who has a life like this? Nobody, that's who." The owl screeched, again, and it sounded weaker. I stopped climbing for a second and looked up at it. Its foot had gotten tangled in some kind of wire on a metal rung. If it didn't calm down, it would snap its foot in half. "See? I'm a hero. An animal lover. Only an animal lover would do this twice in a lifetime." I had had a run-in with an animal rights organization because of an incident with a snake, and I still got poisoned pen letters from Betty White because of it.

"I'm almost there," I called to the owl. I was huffing and puffing pretty bad, and I wondered if I should ask Bird for a diet before my wedding. She was the owner of the local beauty salon, and she was always on one diet or another. She probably had something that would work in a week. "If you're plastic, I will not finish killing you."

But it wasn't plastic. As I got to the rung underneath it, I could see that it was real. "I'm here to help you, so just keep calm," I told the bird. It screeched in reply and flapped its wings. "I'm being a hero," I reminded it.

I stretched out my arm, and as gently as I could, I tried to extricate the owl's foot from the wire.

There are times in a person's life where they realize they're doing something stupid the moment they do it. The guy who fell off a cliff while taking a selfie probably was one of them. Ditto the guy who used a match to see if he had gas in his truck's gas tank.

And then there was me, trying to save an owl on a

telephone pole.

Surprisingly, the owl's foot came untangled easily, but instead of flying away, it went right for me, hell-bent on revenge. "I'm a hero," I managed right before the owl screeched and attacked me. All I saw was beak and feathers before it was on me. I waved my hands at it, trying to protect myself, clenching my thighs tight around the pole.

I stayed up for about three seconds, which felt like hours, as I battled against the bird, who obviously blamed me for getting stuck on the pole.

Life is so unfair.

I was vaguely aware of the sound of sirens coming closer, but I was focused on survival. I was looking at either death by owl or death by sidewalk. It was a tossup which was better, but my body decided for me. I grabbed the pole, wrapped my arms around it and sat my thighs on the metal rungs. Even though I had stopped swatting at the owl, it continued to fight me, dive-bombing right down my top.

"Sonofabitch!" I screamed with the owl down my shirt. It scraped and clawed at my bra, and I let go of the pole long enough to rip my shirt off and swat the owl away. Gravity took over and I fell backward until I was hanging upside down, watching the owl fly away in victory and my shirt float down to the ground.

Below me, there were a fire truck, two police cars, and one familiar-looking unmarked police car. Spencer got out of the car, holding a megaphone in his hand. He turned it on and put it in front of his mouth.

"Are you kidding me?" he shouted up at me.

Grab your copy of *It's A Wonderful Knife* today!

ABOUT THE AUTHOR

Elise Sax writes hilarious happy endings. She worked as a journalist, mostly in Paris, France for many years but always wanted to write fiction. Finally, she decided to go for her dream and write a novel. She was thrilled when *An Affair to Dismember*, the first in the *Matchmaker Mysteries* series, was sold at auction.

Elise is an overwhelmed single mother of two boys in Southern California. She's an avid traveler, a swing dancer, an occasional piano player, and an online shopping junkie.

Friend her on Facebook: facebook.com/ei.sax.9
Send her an email: elisesax@gmail.com
You can also visit her website: elisesax.com
And sign up for her newsletter to know about new releases and sales: https://bit.ly/2PzAhRx

Made in the USA
Las Vegas, NV
02 July 2022

51020767R00157